DEF[...]

A DRAGONS LOVE CURVES NOVEL

AIDY AWARD

Defy Me

Dragons Love Curves ~ Book Six

Aidy Award

Coffee Break Publishing

DENVER, COLORADO

Aidy Award/Coffee Break Publishing

www.coffeebreakpublishing.com

Publisher's Note: This is a work of fiction. Names, characters, places, and incidents are a product of the author's imagination. Locales and public names are sometimes used for atmospheric purposes. Any resemblance to actual people, living or dead, or to businesses, companies, events, institutions, or locales is completely coincidental.

Cover Design by Melody Simmons

Defy Me/ Aidy Award. -- 1st ed.

ASIN - B07N8JT6GD

ISBN - 978-1-950228-00-3

For every hot man wearing a kilt.

NO SOUL, NO SOULMATE. UNTIL HER...

Jett~

I know full well I don't get to even feel love, much less fall in it.

No soul, no soulmate. Ever.

I don't have room for stolen kisses and fantasies of of making her mine. I've got to break the curse on my brethren and take down the King of Hell.

So why is the dragon part of me insisting on marking and claiming this strange and beautiful woman who just walked into my life (and drank my beer)?

Yvaine~

Really weird stuff is happening, like how I accidentally keep turning this hot guy into a dragon and how I really, really wants to kiss him. Again.

What am I thinking? Dark and broody bad boys with those kind of six-pack abs only want one thing, and they don't want it from me and my big ole butt.

We're stuck together until we can figure out how to break some crazy supernatural curse on me.

But what if I don't want the curse broken?

If you love your shifters broody & hot, your heroines curvy & sassy, and can hardly wait for a feel good Happy Ever After, read this book now!

"Your name is a golden bell hung in my heart.

I would break my body to pieces to call you once by your name."

—Peter S. Beagle

ACKNOWLEDGMENTS

Special thanks to Blue St. James for pushing me to get my books done!

Hugs,
--A

DRAGONS AND OTHER GOOD LUCK CHARMS

*F*ucking dragons.

And their fucking mates. Who were all beautiful brave women each of which he had more than a little crush on. If he hadn't seen what finding a soulmate had done for those stupid Wyvern bastards with his own eyes he wouldn't be such a miserable asshole. Now all he could think about was getting a soul shard, finding a mate, and getting the boost in power that came with. It was the only way to save his brothers.

Save himself.

You do one little favor for the most powerful warriors on the planet and they think your soul is redeemable. No matter how much Jett wanted that to be true, it was never going to happen. He poured himself another drink and downed it, liking the burn. It wasn't as hot as his dragon fire, or as satisfying, but for some gods-forsaken reason he came to this little pub night after night waiting on that damned magic dealer to return and in the meantime, tried to get drunk.

No one here tried to manipulate him or wanted anything

from him. It was nice and quiet and as mind numbing as ancient Latin. For decades, all his years spent in hell, he'd wished for normalcy. Now that he had it, he was miserable. Maybe he should pick a fight. At least that would be better than crying in his Jägermeister.

He couldn't get into it with a human though. They were too damn fragile. How did these stinking animals even survive in a world where monsters, like demon dragons, were real? Where monsters like he himself were real. No, if he wanted to work off some steam, he needed to find one of those creatures of the night.

His senses told him the group at the nearest table had no powers, although one of them seriously looked like an ogre. Most of the people who lived in this little dot on the map that was Glückstadt, Germany were nothing. That's why it was a good place to hide out. A different kind of presence nipped at the edges of his spidey-senses. Something definitely not human, but with the familiar acrid scent of fire and brimstone. He could find the creature and have some fun hunting it. With his parentage there wasn't anything hellborn he couldn't catch. But it might be more entertaining to see what it was doing here, before he killed it.

The door of the pub blew open and a blonde woman with the glow of something supernatural around her rushed in like the wind had shoved her through the doorway. Jett glanced around to see if anyone else in here noticed how she was lit up like a damned star in the gold night sky.

A few patrons looked her way, but only because of the disturbance. None were taken aback by who or what she was. Not that he had a clue what kind of being hid under her skin. He couldn't be the only one seeing her aura of shiny power.

He'd bet a dragon's hoard that whatever beast was here knew and was lying in wait for her.

This should be interesting. Jett picked up his stein and took a long swig, waiting for the scene to play out. If he was lucky, the big bad wolf would make trouble.

The woman pushed her hair out of her face, save one errant strand that she gave a well-practiced blow and then tucked behind her ear. My, oh my. He'd never wanted to be a piece of hair so badly in his life. That mouth was something. She tugged on her t-shirt, that had - shit - a unicorn of all things on it. Any grown woman who wore something like that had an innocence about her that he needed to stay far, far away from.

Her shirt refused to stay in place, and it crept back up, showing the thinnest sliver of skin between it and her jeans. That tiny swathe of her bare side had his cock standing up and taking notice. Which was strange. It wasn't like he had seen, tasted, caressed, and spanked a whole lot more flesh than that.

Jett readjusted his legs, spreading them wide under the table to give his brand new erection some relief from the zipper of his jeans. Then he leaned back in his chair waiting for the action to start. And it would. The masked hell's beast had taken notice of her presence too.

Blondie caught him staring at her and headed straight to his table. Uh-oh. She was going to bring the trouble to him. He'd been laying low for a while, ever since he'd helped Cage, the stupid Gold Wyvern, rescue his mermaid mate from Hell and gotten his own ass kicked by the Black Dragon in the process. Jett would be back for his father's head soon enough. Once he had what he needed to free his brethren.

Blondie made her way through the rest of the patrons and

plonked down in the chair next to him. Not across, not on the other side, but so close his arm brushed up against hers as she picked up his half full mug of beer and took two, three, four long gulping swallows.

His cock once again was jealous of an inanimate object. Jett watched her, fascinated. He didn't exactly radiate friendly, come sit with me vibes. The opposite, if his entire life up until now was any proof.

She plonked the now empty stein down on the table and burped. "Pretend to be my boyfriend." She looked back at the door, then at him, her lavender eyes sparkling. "You know, my big bad, very possessive boyfriend."

He'd never in his life seen anyone with eyes like hers. They were mesmerizing. But not enough that he was willing to do something dumb like try to protect her from whatever was chasing her. "And why would I do that?"

"Don't ask. Just kiss me." She glanced back at the door again and the next second it flew open again. Then she slid her fingers into his hair and planted her lips on his.

Jett caught a glimpse of two men with too many muscles not to be supernatural beings shove their way into the room. And he didn't care even a little bit. She touched her mouth to his and the world exploded into fucking rainbows. There could be dragon warriors come to lop off his head, or the Black Dragon himself hunting him down- none of the above would get him to pay any attention to them. Because this was the best fucking kiss he'd ever experienced in his entire miserable life and all she'd done so far was brush her lips across his in a chaste tease.

Not that he spent a lot of time going around kissing people. He'd spent more of his above ground time with the succubae of Geshtianna's coven trying to lure him into their beds than looking for bed partners of his own. Not a single talented succubus had even come close to blowing his mind like this soft, supple, sweet woman licking over his bottom lip asking him to open for her.

Her eyes fluttered shut and the tiniest whimpered moan from her hit him low and hard in the gut. He wrapped an arm around her waist and pulled her in closer wanting to feel the heat of her body touching his. She was warm and soft, her ample curves molded to his hard angles. His fingers found their way to that bit of skin he'd been dying to touch.

She was so damn soft, so fucking sweet.

He didn't do soft. Or sweet. He took what he wanted, when he wanted it.

But not with her. He would give this woman anything she wanted, any time that she wanted it. He'd give her everything if he could. Not that he had much to give.

The sound of a throat being cleared tried its best to break into Jett's living fantasy. "Ahem."

Damn it. This goddess was mere centimeters away from pushing her tongue into his mouth so he could finally taste her, and some asshole was going to interfere. He would simply have to kill them. He very gently broke the kiss but moved his lips only far enough away from hers to speak. "Go away. We're busy."

Jett breathed in her scent. She was snow and sunshine, morning dew on fluffy kittens. Shit. Where did that even come from? Whatever spell she was working on him had turned his brain into mush. Kittens. He didn't even like Grumpy Cat, much less mewling little fur balls.

Blondie had reopened her eyes, but her lips were parted waiting for him to kiss her once again. He brushed that strand of hair off her face and pushed a hand gently into her locks.

His body said take, but his mind, and something else he couldn't identify, told him to treat her like a fragile glass ornament.

"Ah, Ah, Ahem."

This person did not understand they were endangering their own life. "What part of go away don't you understand?"

The interrupter, who turned out to be the barmaid named Ninsy who always served him here rolled her eyes and whispered, "You two might want to take that somewhere else. Because those mermen are going to throw a whole lot more than cold water on you."

Jett glanced at the men. Mers. He never did like those guys. Way too full of themselves. Hold up. How did the barmaid know they were not just a couple of strong arms? He'd never detected anything supernatural about her. Maybe she was a witch who used a dampening spell.

He'd be rethinking his choice in watering hole if that were true. He had no love for magical women of any kind. Except whatever the woman in his arms was. He still had no idea. Only that he wanted and needed her. Needed to keep her safe. "Come on, sweet thing. Let's get you out of here."

There was a back entrance he'd used a time or two to avoid other supernaturals. His gasthaus wasn't far. They could continue their kiss and he'd do all the fun and naughty things a pretend boyfriend should do to her there.

"Thanks, but you've provided enough of a distraction. Sorry." She shrugged.

"You don't have to apologize. I thoroughly enjoyed it. " In fact, he'd like to do it a whole lot more.

"Oh, I'm not sorry about that." She pecked him on the cheek and then twisted out of his arms and ducked.

A fat scaly fist slammed into his face in the exact spot her lips had been only a second before. He fell backward, bowling over a whole row of wooden barstools. Very few beings got the drop on him. It was how he'd stayed alive in the depths of Hell as long as he had. He laid on the floor for a second, wondering what the fuck had just happened. He'd honed his fighting skills even more than what his demon of a mother had taught him. Living among succubae and incubae wasn't exactly a walk in the park and those blood suckers had been good training partners. Living with a coven of sex slaves was better than feigning that he was a mindless drone under the Black Witch's spell. For example, if he was bespelled he wouldn't be able to do this.

Jett blew a burst of flames at his attacker's face, lighting the merman's blue hair on fire. The damn fool slapped at his head and ran around the pub unwittingly stoking the flames. Dumbass.

Now, where had blondie gone?

An all-out brawl broke out in the pub and if he didn't find her quickly, she might get hurt. He jumped up on top of a table and surveyed the room for her almost luminescent hair and lush body. Aha. There she was. He expected to find her hiding in a corner, but she was moving through the fracas like a ninja. She bobbed and weaved, spinning around, under, and past the fists being thrown.

Not only could the woman kiss, she could move. Not a single punch even came close to her. While everyone else was diving into the fray, she made her way to the door. Except there were two very large burly men engaged in battle in front of the exit. No way she was getting out that way unless he helped her.

Jett jumped over tables and chairs and even considered pulling out his wings to fly over everyone's heads so he could get to her faster. She was within a meter of the men now and it looked even less likely that they were simply going to let her pass. She paused a half a meter away from them and crossed her arms. Behind her a very loud screaming woman jumped on someone else's back and pulled at his hair steering him like a pony right toward blondie.

They were going to barrel into her, and she was standing there staring at the two men blocking the door. Shit. She was trapped and they were all going to collide. She would be crushed. Jett put on a burst of speed and jumped off someone's shoulders flying through the air toward her and the oncoming disaster.

As he careened over the tops of the brawlers, time slowed. Blondie turned and looked up at him, winked and moved toward the men. She reached her hand forward, pulled something out of the bigger of the two men's pocket and slipped between them and out the door.

Jett crashed into the men, who attacked him for breaking in on their fight. It took him a good fifteen minutes to beat them off and extricate himself from the pub. By then there was no sight of his little kissing ninja thief. He didn't need to be able to see her to find her. He had her soft intricate scent. As did whatever other creatures of the night were stalking her.

He rubbed his hands together. The chase was on and it was going to be fun.

DRAGON ASS INN

*W*hew, that was a close one. It had taken Yvaine all day to shake those guys off her tail. If she hadn't needed the money so badly, she would have stuck to less menacing tourists to pick pocket. But with the dreary rain all day, the sight-seers just weren't out and about. She'd run out of funds yesterday, or was it the day before? Either way, she hadn't eaten in a million years and those two guys didn't seem to mind standing around in the rain. They also hadn't even tried to secure their wallets. It was like they'd never been outside their own homes before, but they spoke a language that was far from German, Spanish, or English and the pickings were just too easy.

She hated stealing. But she also hated sleeping in the rain and eating trash. She did what she had to--she survived.

Except they'd caught her. Which was a new one. Yvaine could lift a wallets like a Charles Dickens street urchin. Sure, lots of people had that skill. Her super power was that they never ever noticed. She could take their cash and replaced their wallet before they caught on. She knew first-hand how much it sucked to not have any form of ID when far from home, family, or friends.

Not that she had a family. Or friends. Or a home.

No one had ever taught her to pick pocket. No, she'd learned really useful skills like reciting Hail Marys and Our Fathers while getting her knuckles rapped for sharing her porridge with the new kid who'd come to breakfast too late to get his own portion.

Fucking porridge.

She'd been about ten seconds from being caught by them when that little pub had called to her like lighthouse in a storm. Like literally. Out of all the businesses in the alley, that one had shined like a black light at a rave into the cloudy, murky evening. She'd learned to trust a gift like that, even if she didn't understand. Running into the broody hunka-hunka burning love was an added bonus. He'd saved her ass too. In more ways than he knew.

Not only had he unwittingly helped her escape, he was also paying for a warm place to sleep tonight and the biggest veggie burger and fries she could find. She pulled out the cash from the wallet she'd lifted off of him. There hadn't been time to slip it back. She'd blame that on the kiss. The one that had distracted her so much she almost hadn't cared if she gotten caught.

She tossed the rest of the contents into the nearest trash can. Couldn't be a litter bug. What kind of person carries three-thousand euros around in his wallet? He didn't look like some rich entitled trust fund baby. He barely looked like he'd bathed in the last week. He'd sure tasted good though. Spicy, like hot cinnamon. She touched her lips remembering the feeling of his mouth on hers.

She could check first kiss off the list.

A shiver that she enjoyed a little too much snuck across the fine hairs on the back of her neck.

Or maybe that was the touch of snow beginning to fall.

Must be the snow.

The other wallet had only a couple of euros, but it had a Eurail pass that would sure come in handy. After a good night sleep and something to eat... mmm pastries and wiessbier, she was getting the hell out of here. This town was done for her and she hadn't found any clues or answers anyway. Calling themselves the luck town was like false advertising. It was just plain dumb to stick around any longer.

Now to find a place to stay tonight. She walked a little faster putting more distance between her and the bar brawl. The crisp night air felt good whipping through her hair, like she was running in a wide open field. Not that she spent a lot of time running. Well, not the jogging kind anyway. Only the away and hiding kind of running. She shouldn't be out in the open like this right now anyway. She'd had that sickening feeling of being watched for far too long to ignore it.

"Hey - you. Come back here you little thief."

She didn't wait to see if it was the two men she'd been running from already or the man she'd kissed. Either party was going to be pissed. Time to go. Again.

She bolted off the main square and down a maze of cobbled streets. She couldn't run for long before she'd run out of steam, so she needed to find a place to duck into and hide in the next twenty seconds. She headed toward an area advertising hostels and gasthauses. Since it wasn't tourist season, most of them should have a private room vacant for her. She passed two hostels that looked a bit too run down for her to feel secure staying there and then spotted one she didn't remember seeing before. It had one of those old-school wooden signs swinging above the doorway. A big dragon was carved into the wood and painted with at least twenty brilliant colors.

A quick glance over her shoulder and she didn't see her pursuer anywhere. Good, she was already holding her side and gulping in air. A dark shadow blipped through the corner of her peripheral vision. But not on the street or by one of the buildings. It had been up on the rooftop. Must be some kind of a bird, although a big one. An owl or a bat.

Her shoulders involuntarily shook. Whatever it was, it gave her the creeps. She needed to get inside immediately if not sooner.

"Well, don't stand out there all night, sugar. Come in and get warm. I've got gluhwein on the stove." The most beautiful woman Yvaine had ever seen smiled and held open the door to the little inn and waved her inside.

Hmm. The woman was too friendly by half. More than the normal business hawker. Why? What did she want from Yvaine besides her money? Everyone out here in the real world always wanted something from her.

This small inn did feel safer than any other place to stay on the block. She wasn't sure why. She trusted her instincts and so far, they had kept her from being taken advantage of. But she was getting really mixed signals here. Safety, weirdness, calm vibes, but also the sense of someone who was ready for a fight. Which was extra strange, because this woman was soft and curvy with long mother-nature with flowing hair and a soft smile. Not exactly the warrior type.

A tall, very handsome man, who reminded her of Jason Momoa, but with a prosthetic arm stuck his head out the door and over the woman's shoulder. "Ooh, you found her."

Yvaine took a big ole step back. Uh-oh. She'd gotten really

good at hiding these past few months. She did not want to be found by anyone. Who were these people? Who was looking for her? She narrowed her eyes at the couple and opened her mouth to tell them thanks, but no thanks.

Instead of words coming out, she burped. Holy hell. There was that beer she'd downed back to haunt her. It wasn't just that though. A gurgle sounded from her belly and nausea roiled.

The woman rolled her eyes and waved the guy off. "Don't mind my mate. He means I found a paying customer. It's been a slow week."

Mate? She must mean husband. Right? Yvaine's vision went a little fuzzy and she couldn't quite think straight. Husband. That was a weird word. Huzz. Band.

The woman wrapped her arm around Yvaine's shoulder and guided her toward the front door.

"I have a very nice room all ready for you. Big comfy bed, plenty of space, and black out curtains so no one will be able to see in. " She winked. "And we'll get you fed too. Soak up some of that beer."

Yvaine had a super weird vibe from these two, but not uncomfortable. That sent a four-alarm fire worth of warnings off in her head. Something was wrong. Trust no one.

A shot of adrenaline hit her right in the heart, pumping through her veins like a cold shower, clearing her head. She still felt unsteady on her feet and that doorway was looking very enticing, if only to lean on.

Holy hell. She'd been drugged. The inn keepers hadn't even touched her. It couldn't be them.

The beer.

But Mr. McBroodypants hadn't known she was coming or that she'd pick up his drink and down it. Which meant someone had been trying to drug him. That didn't seem plausible either. She couldn't imagine what anyone would do with a big muscle-y passed-out dude like him. She was back to the couple looking at her expectantly from the shelter of their doorway. Yvaine wavered on her feet again.

The flash of darkness flew overhead again and even the woman lifted her eyes to the sky. "Come on, dear. It's getting dark out."

Uh. It was nine o'clock at night. In the winter. It had been dark for hours. One more reason she should keep on running. Except for that very distinct feeling she was being watched. Hunted. By something malevolent. Her head wasn't on straight and if she did look for another place to take shelter, she couldn't even guarantee she would make it another block down the street.

Either she went inside and hoped for the best that these people weren't responsible for her current state of weirdness, or she risked being seen by the watcher, or worse captured by her pickpocket victims, or the thing that was definitely not a bat.

Two, or was it three, sucky choices. What was new?

Her body decided for her, because she lost her footing and pitched forward. Her vision tunneled, but she refused to lose consciousness. The man caught her and swooped his prosthetic arm under her knees, lifting her up, and carried her inside. The door slammed shut behind them.

The room was warm and comforting and the cold that had seeped into her lifted a smidge. It would be so easy to just close her eyes and fall asleep right here in these big strong arms. Strong arms that could protect her, keep her safe.

Yvaine shook her head. No no no. She was the only one

who could keep herself safe. "I'm okay. You can put me down now."

To her surprise, he did, holding his hands out on either side of her like she was a toddler just learning to walk. "You all right there, kiddo?"

"Yeah. Fine. Thanks. Just tired." She was hella tired and still woozy. She'd feel better after she ate. "Do you have room service by any chance?"

"No need for that. Your dinner is all ready." The woman indicated to a coffee table in front of a fireplace. On a tray in the middle was what looked like a veggie burger, fries, a huge green salad, a plateful of pastries, and a bubbling glass of weissbeir. Yum.

She plopped down into the nearest chair and tucked right in. Mmm. She couldn't even remember the last time she'd had fresh veggies like this, and the burger must be some secret blend of twelve herbs and spices because it was like crack cocaine it was so delicious.

"I think you over spelled her, heart of my heart. She nearly passed out."

"Desperate times. He was circling. We couldn't let him get to her."

That sure sounded like they were talking about her. "Crphrn't frnt whew?"

"Don't talk with your mouth full, dearest."

Grr. She hated being told what to do. Fine. She chewed, swallowed and took another bite. This one slightly smaller so she could be understood while talking with her mouth full. "Couldn't." Chew. "Let." Chew chew. "Who?"

"You aren't supposed to be able to hear us talking about you. That's strange." The woman looked at her husband and frowned. "Did you do something to her?"

Yeah. Did he?

He shook his head. "Nope. That's all her, babe. I told you she was special."

Yvaine narrowed her eyes and popped a couple of fries into her mouth watching the interaction between them. She wasn't entirely sure why she wasn't getting up and Houdini-ing her way out of here. The things they were saying... she should be afraid, very afraid. She wasn't even a little bit. Possibly for the first time in her entire life.

Maybe it was the drugs, maybe it was that she was exhausted from being on the run and not finding the answers she'd been looking for and with no end in sight.

Probably that one.

The woman folded her arms unconvinced and glanced at Yvaine. She waved her hands at the pile of french fries that were almost gone. More appeared. Literally bottomless fries. Rock on.

"I can see that she is. But are you sure she's the one?" The woman looked Yvaine up and down, like she was trying to figure out who - or what - she was.

Just an orphan looking for answers. Nothing else. Nothing to see here. Yvaine ate another fry. "The one what?"

The woman frowned. "Stop doing that."

The man got a big ole grin and Yvaine had the feeling he didn't get the one up on his wife very often. "Yes. She's the only one. Give it to her."

Whatever it was, Yvaine wanted it. Badly. Why? Jiminy Cricket, this whole situation was like a dream. She stood up and extended her hand, waiting for the woman to give her the it.

"Fine." The woman wrinkled her nose and lifted a super shiny and sparkly necklace from under the neckline of her dress. She dangled the chain in the air and then laid it over Yvaine's head. It sparked like it was electric and a bright white light filled the room for the blink of an eye.

"Whoa. What did you give me?" Yvaine lifted the charm from her chest and stared down at it. It was a shiny black dragon with a bright pink and green thistle wrapped around it. Pretty.

"I'm still not sure this is a good idea, but sometimes we do things we don't want to for the ones we love." The woman sighed and the man wrapped his arm around her and kissed her on the top of the head.

"Thank you, love. You'll see, it will work out. He's got good in him even if you don't believe it yet. He must."

Yvaine yawned. The crazy day, a full belly, and weird people had taken their toll. She was going to sleep like a rock for the first time in ages. "I guess I should check in and pay you for the room and the dinner."

The woman shook her head. "You scoot on upstairs. We'll take care of the rest in the morning."

"'Kay." She trudged up the stairs and walked into the first open room she found. She laid her bag on the floor next to a big fluffy bed that was totally calling her name. Wait, when had she gotten her bag? She'd left it in a locker at the bus station where she'd slept the last two nights.

Seriously. She must already be asleep because this night was too weird not to be made up by her subconscious. She longed for a safe place and her mind must have created one. She'd think about that tomorrow. For a little while longer she wanted to bask in the warmth of magical unending french fries and feeling protected.

The voices of the couples drifted into her room as she was crawling into bed.

"He stole a shard, Kur. Messed up a whole lot of well laid plans. Besides, I don't have to do anything for him, he's not mine. I don't even have to like him, and you can't make me." She sounded pretty mad.

"Sweetness," The man crooned. "He's my blood."

"He's your bastard."

Ooh - somebody was in trouble. But they actually seemed like a pretty solidly in love couple.

"He's the key."

The key. The key. The word rolled around in Yvaine's mind like a song stuck in there. When she closed her eyes and drifted off the key was flying, like a bird through the sky. No, not a bird. A dragon. A beautiful black gleaming dragon that breathed fire. She ran and ran and ran, trying to catch it. That was her key. Her dragon.

Yvaine awoke with a start. Something scratching at her window had startled her out of her sleep. She crept over to the dark curtains and pushed them open the tiniest of cracks. Early morning light poured in. She opened them further and saw only a few people making their way to wherever they were going. Nothing that would have made that sound. Especially not up on the second floor.

She'd slept through the night. A quick glance around the room found it still secure, her bag on the floor, her clothes except for her t-shirt in a heap beside it. She grabbed up her jeans and pulled the wad of bills out of her pocket. It was all still there along with the Eurail pass. Something had gone right for a change.

Please let that little bit of good luck continue. She quickly dressed and headed downstairs, ready to pay for her room and get out as fast as she could. Gone was the coffee table where she'd sat and eaten last night, and there wasn't even a fireplace. No beautiful woman or good-looking man stood behind the desk either. A young woman in a World Cup t-shirt sat on a stool, snapping her gum and reading a magazine.

Well, she couldn't expect that the couple worked all hours. Maybe this was their daughter, or just some hired help. Yvaine went to the desk to pay.

"Hi, I owe for one night in a private room."

"We don't have private rooms. What's your name? I'll look you up. You're lucky if you didn't have to share with anyone last night. We were almost full up."

"Oh. Uh. Look under van den Hoogenbond. Amy."

"Naw. We definitely don't have anyone registered under that name."

"Can you look again?" Of course, the girl wasn't going to find anything. But she clacked away on the computer and Yvaine slid a hundred Euro note out of the folds and slipped it onto the counter. Before the girl looked up from her search, Yvaine was already out the door and headed toward the train station.

She stopped by a food cart to grab a cup of something hot and some breakfast. She wished she'd grabbed one of the pastries from the dinner plate last night and saved if for this morning. If there had even been a dinner. She wasn't convinced.

"Ein cafe und diese...uh, pastries." Her German was pretty crap, but the guy got the gist when she pointed to some chocolate croissants.

A deep voice that send shivers down her spine said from behind her, "Make that two coffees and add in some of those sausage rolls. The lady is buying."

Yvaine spun around and was face to face with the large muscle-bound chest of Mr. McBroodypants himself.

COME OUT, COME OUT WHEREVER YOU ARE

*I*t hadn't taken him more than a few minutes to extricate himself from the brawl at the pub, but by the time he got out to the street, his little thief was gone. Disappeared into the night. That was okay, because Jett was the night.

He slipped into the shadow of a building and let the darkness envelope him, show him its secrets. The demon inside stretched and reveled in the cool night air. This was a part of himself he kept buried, unused, unacknowledged. He hated how its base instincts tried to control him.

It couldn't any longer. Jett knew better now. Tonight he'd let the animal out of its cage to help him hunt the girl.

He sniffed the air and caught a whiff of sulfur first. A minion of hell was nearby. The scent faded under a waft of something much more potent. Sunshine. At midnight dark thirty. The demon recoiled at the scent. It took a long time to train himself to be out in the light of day. He still preferred the dark. Even more when he was in search of prey.

Delicious, mouth-watering prey. That he was going to devour. Eat her right up. Until she screamed his name.

A heartbeat thrummed nearby, and another. The musk of lust wafted to him a moment before a couple walking hand in hand turned the corner. They didn't see him, but likely sensed his presence because they hurried on their way faster than before.

Or maybe they were just anxious to get home and into each other's pants.

He scented the air again, searching for the bit of sunshine that his thief smelled of. The unique flavor of her was part of what made him want her so much.

The demon was drawn to several more hearts pushing blood through the weak little bodies of the humans. It couldn't help but want a snack. Jett kept it satisfied with very rare steak. Tonight he ignored it. He wanted something entirely different. An ache he hadn't allowed himself to feel for a hundred years mawed open in his chest.

Only she could fill it.

Jett shook his head. What the fuck kind of thinking was that? He had never needed anything or anyone. Ever. This was a passing fancy. A wild goose chase, a lark. Something to entertain him for a few hours while he awaited news from the magic dealer. The fucking really well-paid man who had so far come up with nothing but fairy tales.

He couldn't save his brethren with rainbows and unicorn kisses.

Unicorn blood on the other hand...

Jett let himself sink into the shadow and his form dissolve. He shifted into his demon dragon form, his senses reaching out and touching every bit of life in the area. He could feel the blood rushing through everything from the sleeping tourists in the buildings around him to the tiniest cockroach under their beds.

She had to be here somewhere. His dragon sight took over and he jumped onto the rooftops. He would be able to better track her from up here. There. Over in an alleyway, he could taste her in the shadows. He followed the scent up and down the narrow spaces between buildings. She was here, but she wasn't.

He hadn't thought she was a witch. She was something, but magic like that had a particular flavor about it. He'd met several witches, both powerful and not. None of them had the deliciousness of his thief. Now, where could she be.

Jett set his nose to the rooftop tiles and followed any hint of her scent. She was here, he knew it. He peaked in windows and saw plenty of beautiful women in various states of undress. He couldn't care less. None of them were the one he sought. None of them were her.

Obsessed much? His search was bordering on it. This was more than a mere distraction now. He couldn't do anything but sit around and drink beer until he got the next clue in his quest to kill the Black Dragon and break the curse.

He relished a good distraction. She was it--his new goal.

Hours passed with no progress and soon the sun would lighten the sky. He wouldn't be able to hide in the shadows much longer. Being seen in dragon form would only stir up trouble. Fine. He would shift back to his human form. Eventually she'd have to come out of her hiding place, and he would be ready to pounce on her.

Jett slid down the side of the building he stood on, sneaking into the last shadows of the night. A swirl of black wafted around his feet. He wasn't the only creature of the dark. Against the wall, a demon dragon, his brethren formed out of the inky blackness.

One of the demon dragon's wings was torn nearly off and he had deep cuts crisscrossing his body. Jett recognized those wounds. They were from his father's fire whip. The King of Hell himself had beaten one of his brothers, nearly to death.

"Jett." Its hissed voice was a mere rasp, telegraphing the pain. "AllFather comes. Jett dies. Go now."

His brother collapsed and Jett caught him in his arms. The dcmon dragon's head lulled and there was no saving him. Damn it all to the fiery pits.

"Rest now brother and know no more pain."

Black eyes, matching Jett's own blinked up at him one more time. "Jett comes. AllFather dies."

The cursed creature turned to coal black dust, staining the wall, the street, and Jett's skin.

Jett could do nothing but growl low and re-avow the vengeance he would wreak for this death. More of his brothers died, mostly killed by the dragons he'd stuck a pseudo-alliance with or his own father's hand. He may have clawed his way out of hell, but it followed him each and every day. It would continue to until he could return and depose his father, end his reign.

Only then would he and his brothers be free. To do that he needed an army of his own. He'd tried already to battle the Black Dragon on his own. He would have died trying if the dragons would have let him. But, no. They had to rescue someone else's fated mates.

Fuck fate.

At least he'd extracted a future favor from the Gold Dragon Wyvern in the process. Once he had the key to ending the curse, he'd call in the favor. Big time.

Until then, he needed to keep a low profile. If his father had found him in this seaside German village, it was time to find a new village. Maybe in the south of France. He'd had a shameful lack of sunshine in his life.

Jett wiped his hands clean and glanced around to make sure no other demon dragons were about. Only the cursed could be trusted. The others were dumb as fucking boxes of rocks and would report his position back to his father hoping for a boon.

He neither saw or sensed any darkness rising. What he did get was a slap in the face of her. That unique energy that was entirely the little thief was amped up and calling to him like a giant flashing sign that said, "Come and get me."

Well, fuck. No woman, lickable or not, was worth risking his life or the lives he was responsible for. So why wasn't he walking away? What was it that had him chasing her all night long and rooted now to this spot watching her like a creepy stalker?

She walked out of the front of a building he'd searched a half-dozen times last night. An electrified magical charm winked at him from her chest, dangling on a delicate chain around her throat. She had not been wearing that last night.

Zings of energy, lust, and the need to claim her as his own burst every damn cell in his body, filling him with light and intense need. No way, no how could he leave her to the destruction the Black Dragon was about to wreak on this little town.

Death if he stayed, death to her if he didn't. Caught between a rock and a hard on. He wasn't as dumb as he looked. Jett was going to have the best of both worlds if he acted fast. His enticing thief was standing at a food cart and he snuck up behind her. She was fumbling with some awkward German.

"Ein cafe und diese...uh, pastries." She pointed to some chocolate croissants.

Adorable.

Blech. He'd never in his life thought anything was adorable.

For some insane reason every time he looked at her his brain went all fluffy. His cock was anything but - no, it was rock fucking hard. Just from seeing her lick her lips in antici-pation of a sweet treat for breakfast. He'd really like to lick that chocolate off her lips. "Make that two coffees and add in some of those sausage rolls. The lady is buying."

She spun around and Jett thoroughly enjoyed seeing the shock on her face and her perusal of his chest. He even found himself puffing up for her. Which was ridiculous. The vendor handed over the rolls and Jett slapped a few bills on the table. It wasn't like he didn't have plenty. What she'd taken was a pittance.

He grabbed the bag and cups, handing her one even while her mouth continued to open and close like a funny little fish. "How, what, I--"

Jett slid his hand into the soft small of her back, just above her plump rear end and guided her away from the cart. Funny how they fit together perfectly like this. "I'm not going to hurt you, but there are those who will. You need to come with me before the real bad guys show up."

"I don't need your help." She tried to jerk away but stiff-ened and then stilled entirely. Her eyes went wide as pancakes and her jaw dropped.

Jett looked up to where she was staring and swore. Right then, those bad guys he'd warned her about showed up.

The sky darkened with unnatural storm clouds darkened the early morning sky. Demon dragons popped up in the new shadowed corners right there on the street. Damn, the Black Dragon was growing fucking bold to send his minions out among the humans in broad daylight. They couldn't do that on their own, which meant, the asshole himself really was on his way.

"Ack. What are those?" His beauty came back to her senses and pointed at a growing puff of black not a foot away in the underbelly of the food cart. That black smoke would soon become one of his brethren.

They would have orders to recapture him and those on his side would not be able to disobey with the Black Dragon so close. He would have to fight them off. Shit. If he was lucky, he could kill a few of the minions and chase the others away.

Enough of his brothers had died in the battles with the dragon warriors. Even more since his own escape from hell. Their deaths were on his head. He wouldn't have anymore.

He pushed the girl behind him and rolled his shoulders ready for the brawl but did not shift even his claws into dragon form. He would take the beating before killing any of the cursed.

"Come on, you dummy." She grabbed his hand and yanked him toward the center of the square that was not yet fully dark but was filling with people. "Don't wait for trouble to find you."

She jerked him away from the burgeoning form of the demon dragon. Jett's arm just about pulled out of his socket before his feet caught up with her. Geez, she was fast. Unexpectedly fast. Whatever kind of being she was hiding behind her human facade had some giddy up and go. He struggled to keep up as she zigged and zagged through the people scurrying around. It wasn't hard to track the demon dragons coming after them, the screams were evidence enough that the bastards were gaining on them.

"Over there." She switched directions and tugged his arm dragging him into hard right. She was heading toward a dark alley.

Yeah, that wasn't going to happen. That way would be teeming with both friends and enemies with no room to tell the difference in a battle. The Black Dragon may be ready to expose them all to world, but Jett wasn't. He needed to get someplace secluded but not dark to shift into his dragon form and fly the two of them away from here.

Before they reached the alley, he shoved her into the open entryway to the last building. It was airy and bright, too fucking bright. Jett held his hand up over his eyes to block the glare of the hundreds of lightbulbs. He had to go and choose escape in a fucking lamp store.

"*Guten Tag. Womit kann ich Ihnen behilflich sein?*" A human male spoke, but Jett growled at him and he scurried away.

"Babe, do you see a stairwell? We need to go up to the rooftop." Babe. He didn't even know her name, but the nickname tasted good on his lips.

"I am not your babe and no I don't see any stairs. We don't want to go up anyway. We'd be trapped on the roof." She gripped his wrist blocking out the glaring light, soothing his already tender skin with only her touch. "What is wrong with you? Why are you covering your face? Did they get you?"

"No, I'm fine. Look again, if we can get to the roof I can get us out of here, away from the demon dragons."

"Oh no. Did you get bonked on the head when I wasn't looking? Because unless you're Richy Rich and have a helicopter waiting at your beck and call, we're going to have to make a run for it. I'm pretty sure I can get us through that crowd."

Damn the light was piercing his brain. Enough. He'd just have to tell her what he was and hope that didn't freak her the fuck out. Or not. "I don't know what you are, and you don't have to tell me if you're not ready to reveal your form, but unless you're prepared to deal with the Black Dragon himself, we have to get out of here now. I can shift and fly us someplace safe."

"Dude. I don't have any idea what you're talking about and we're running out of options. Those things are gathering around the front of the store and they've got rocks."

Rocks? Something whipped past his head and glass smashed in a sickening tinkle. He tried uncovering his eyes, but the glare from the bulbs seared into his brain. "Look. Either we find a way to get up to the roof or I shift here and now in the middle of this store, breaking all these fucking lightbulbs of death and those are the only thing keeping the demon dragons at bay."

He should just do that anyway. Why was he still screwing around with her? He could shift, scare the shit out of the demon dragons, the cursed would back off, and he could fly away. He would, if it wasn't for the way her touch and her voice and the promise of more time in her company, possibly kissing her again kept him by her side.

He was fucking pussy-whipped and he hadn't even seen her with her clothes off yet. He was such a douche. Another rock whizzed through the air, then another and another. Glass shattered and his girl screamed. Fuck if he was letting any of that glass cut into her pearlescent skin marring it before he got to run his tongue over every inch of her.

Eyes be damned. He would heal. Jett squinted blocking as

much of the light out as he could and scanned the room. Fuck, it was like looking directly as the center of the sun. He was already seeing spots in his vision. The demon dragons were strategically taking out the lamps in a path to get to where he and the girl were near the cashier's desk. That was too smart a move for regular demon dragons. Which meant his brethren were directing the battle.

That was either good, because they would let him get away, or very, very bad if the Black Dragon was close enough to be directing it himself. Jett couldn't take the risk of negotiating with them, not with this fragile being by his side.

Said fragile being picked up a shard of glass and hurled it frisbee style slicing off the nearest demon dragon's head. It turned to a stain on the ground and the others backed away. There, in the center of the pack was one of his cursed brothers, scowling at Jett.

"Jett comes, AllFather dies. Why Jett no comes?" His brother threw a rock directly at Jett which barely missed him hitting a chandelier behind them.

Ah, shit.

"Uh... is that thing talking to you?"

Yes. "No. Come on. We're leaving." Jett lifted his girl in a fireman's carry, throwing her over his shoulder so he could shade his eyes with his other hand. Not to mention he got to grasp her with his arm wrapped around her plump ass. Which she wriggled.

"Put me down." She pounded on his back, but only for a moment. "Scratch that. Run, run, run."

What had to be a mountain of glass erupted behind him and Jett felt her press her face and arms into his back. He turned sideways using his body to block the majority of the shards from hitting her. The front of the store went dark and demon dragons swarmed in. Yeah. Time to run.

Jett bolted into the maze of lamps toward the back of the store squinting, searching, trying find anything that could be an exit or a stairwell. This was a tall building, four stories at least. There had to be a way up. If all else failed he was ready to burn through the wall until he found one.

"Dude, hurry up, they're gaining on us."

Okay - fire it is. Jett let the magic that allowed him to shift bubble up just enough that he could send a fireball shooting across the room at the nearest wall. That opened up the wall into a neighboring shop filled with kitchen and bathroom fixtures. Some of which he'd melted.

"You missed, dummy."

He jumped up onto the nearest table and shot another ball of fire at the back wall. That sent the fire alarm off and water squirting from the ceiling. Aha. The stairs. Light poured in but already Jett saw puff of smoke rolling up from the darkness inside the stairwell. They had maybe ten seconds before demon dragons manifested there.

He dove into the darkness, finally able to see again, minus the burns in his retinas and took the stairs two at a time, three, five, until he was bounding up entire flights.

Screeches and screams echoed off the cement walls in such a cacophony that he couldn't tell from which direction the demon dragons were coming at them from. Probably above and below. They only had one more level to get to the roof. They were almost there.

Two dark shadows deepened right in front of the door leading outside. Red eyes of fire peered at him through the darkness. "Jett comes. Now."

He screeched to a halt and the girl squeaked as she banged

into his back hard. "Ouch. Don't stop, they're still coming after us."

Jett slowly slid her down his body and back to her feet. He relished every second of having her body pressed to his, feeling her shirt ride up and his hands slipping across the skin of her sides. This might be the last and only chance he'd have to touch her. Because they were probably about to get dragged to hell.

"Sorry about dragging you into this, little thief. I swear I'll do my best to--" To what? Keep her safe? He'd already failed at that. Rescue her from hell? He was going to need rescuing himself. He didn't know how to finish that sentence, so he didn't. Instead he bent his head down, hoping she wouldn't pull away. If he was going to die, or worse, he wanted his last good memory to be of kissing her.

She was biting her bottom lip and he so wanted to help her with that. "Kiss me, babe. It may be the last thing we do."

"Yvaine."

"Not in vain. A memory we'll be able to hold onto in the depths of hell."

"No, dummy, my name is Yvaine." She lifted up on her tiptoes and pressed her lips to his, sneaking the tip of her tongue into his mouth.

Yvaine moaned into his mouth and he speared his hands into her hair, holding her to him, groaning his own pleasure back to her. The world around them exploded into a black light, tinged with red streaks, but he barely noticed. Maybe it was his brethren spewing fire, maybe they'd blown up the whole building trying to get to him. He didn't care. He only knew now that whoever and whatever his beautiful Yvaine was, she was his savior, and he would die protecting her.

ATTACK OF THE KILLER BATSTRICHES

$\mathcal{W}$ hew. If ever there was not a time to get kissed off her feet, this was it. Yvaine knew better. Didn't she? Apparently not. Because she wanted nothing more than to spend the next few minutes of their probably short lives with her mouth mashed to this man's. Who cared if weird scary monsters were about to eat them? At least she'd die happy. A virgin, but if this was as close as she was going to ever get to being deflowered, she'd take it. God, he felt, and tasted, and smelled, and did she say felt, really good. Like magical.

"Jett comes now." One of the creatures growled and stepped closer. A few more steps and they would be well and truly trapped. They couldn't go back, but they were so close to the door to the roof she could practically taste the freedom.

There was still the tiniest sliver of light between the monsters, the door, and her chance to get away. She could too. She could slip right between them and none of them would even notice until it was too late.

And leave Jett behind.

She liked that name. It suited him. Those black eyes, his dark demeanor, that bad boy in a black leather jacket vibe that was so damn attractive. Everything about him was so broody and sexy. Which shouldn't matter a damn bit. So why wasn't she already running away?

Damn if Yvaine knew. But she wasn't going to leave him.

Which meant he was going to find out about all her weirdness. He already saw her pick pockets, but that was just a skill she'd learned, picked up out of necessity. Escape was like her super power, like good parking karma or knowing exactly when an avocado was perfectly ripe. It wasn't something she ever revealed to anyone. Ever.

Her pseudo-super power was the only reason she was still alive today and how she'd gotten all the way to Germany without them finding her. She didn't know who they were, just that they'd been hunting her. Someone or something was always flippin' after her.

She'd known this guy for all of twelve hours, ten of which she'd been either running away from him or asleep. No way she could trust him with a secret this big. Because what if he was from the They or part of a secret government agency who would want to dissect her and find out how she ticked?

No was he was a G-man. A t-shirt, jeans, and more than a couple days of scruff weren't exactly the standard issue uniform for a super-secret sneaky spy. James Bond this guy was not and Yvaine was no Bond girl.

He brushed his lips ever so gently across hers and whispered against her mouth. "Stay behind me. If they take us to hell, do your best to hide in the caverns. I will come for you."

Uh, hell? No. Yvaine was ready to admit there were some things beyond her explanation, like her own escape artist abilities. She'd seen too many weird things since she'd left the convent not to believe, but actual heaven and hell. Naw. He meant like a horrible prison or something. He couldn't possibly mean actual hell. That wasn't a real thing.

The evidence of monsters from hell in front of her aside. He was being one-hundo percent serious. Yvaine cringed her mind not allowing what she was seeing and experiencing to coalesce with the idea of the supernatural actually existing.

Plus, Jett had said to hide in caverns. The thought of being in an enclosed underground space gave her the heebie jeebies. Being locked up like that would be hell.

That settled that. The two of them were getting out of this. Trust him? She had no choice now. Either giving that up to him would come back to bite her on the ass or... Wow. Two good kisses with a hot guy totally out of her league and her mind was so far into the gutter she was filthy-licious.

Jett tried to shove Yvaine behind him but she pulled him in close, wrapping her arms around his neck so she could whisper into his ear. "Listen. I can't explain, but let them come closer. I can get us out of this, but you have to trust me and never let go of my hand."

She'd only helped someone else escape once before and look how badly that had worked out.

Jett's brow wrinkled and he shook his head already denying her request. They were rapidly running out of time and if he didn't trust her she wasn't sure what would happen. All she knew was that she was getting out of here and she wanted him to come with her.

Want wasn't the right word or feeling. There was a strange tug somewhere in the vicinity of the necklace - just over her heart. But it was coming from inside and accompanied by a real sense of need. Not like the need for chocolate croissants and coffee, or even the need to sleep when she was exhausted from running. This was so much stronger, deeper. She needed Jett to come with her. She needed him to trust.

There was no time to examine why she felt so strongly about him. Later. She'd think about that later. She slid her hand down his arm and slipped her hand into his.

He gripped her hand tight but was still trying to put himself between her and the monsters. "No way. I won't let them hurt you. I don't want to kill any of them, but I will protect you."

Of course, he didn't believe her. He had no reason to. As long as he didn't let go of her hand her weird little super power would take over anyway and they'd get away safely. What happened after that?

He wasn't freaked out by these crazy ass monsters, maybe he wouldn't even care that she was a mutant. Not like she was the badass X-men kind that could fight crime. She was nowhere cool enough to be a villain either. She was just flat out weird. None of what he thought mattered anyway. It wasn't like she was planning on marrying him, having his adorable AF babies, and living happily ever after with him.

Nope. None of that had even crossed her mind. Not at all. God, she was so lame.

She'd get them out of here, maybe kiss the bejesus out of him one more time and they could go their separate ways. After they got away, she'd continue her search for her past and he'd, uh, fly away into the sunset in his helicopter or whatever. Yes. Fine. Time to make that happen. Jett probably wasn't going to like how she did it. Big tough guys didn't like being rescued by the damsel in distress.

Yvaine spun around to face the monsters, put her thumbs in her ears with her fingers splayed like antlers and stuck out her tongue at them. "Nanny, nanny, boo boo. You ca-an't get me."

The two monsters approaching them looked at her like she was a crazy bitch. Jett probably was too. She'd happily take that tiny moment of surprise and use it to her advantage. She grabbed Jett's hand again, flipped the internal switch in her mind that made her invisible as far as she could tell and ran straight toward the bad guys dragging her new partner in crime along behind her.

"Holy shit, babe. What the fuck are you doing to us?" Jett squeezed her hand tighter. She needed all her concentration to get them through the mass of scaly black bat-man things, so she couldn't reply or even examine what his tone meant right now. She'd have to file it away for later to see if he was shocked, in awe, humored, or scared.

She zigged and zagged through the monsters, pulling Jett along behind her. One of the monsters sniffed the air and blew out stinky puffs of smoke right in her face. Step by step they worked their way up the stairs, carefully picking a path through to freedom. Red eyes darted around looking for her and the two that had come for Jett flapped their wings and squawked like some sort of giant evil ostrich-bat hybrids. More squeals sounded from the stairwell behind them and darts of fire shot through the small space.

Great. Fire spitting evil batstriches. Yeah. If Jett wasn't fazed by these creatures, he probably wouldn't blink twice about her Houdini act. She'd done her best to guide him out of the danger zone, but enough was enough. No way she was letting either of them go up in flames. She kicked it into high gear and yanked Jett through the door to the roof.

They busted through the exit, leaving the things in the stairwell flapping around looking for them. Except the roof was no safe zone. The sky had gone almost completely black with ominous clouds and if there was a helicopter coming for them, it would have to land on top of, and hopefully squish, about a hundred more monsters. They covered the roof like a summer dance party.

"Who the hell started a batstrich coop up here?" Crap. She knew this was a bad idea. Where were they supposed to go now? She really didn't want to go back down the stairs.

Jett halted them in their tracks, out of the path of several batstriches scuffling with each other. "Fuck me. He's sent every god-damned demon dragon after me."

"After you?" After him? Wait, they were after him? No way. Why?

"Yeah. We have to get out of here fast. I hope that spell of yours is still working and you aren't afraid of heights."

The wide-open space above them quashed any feelings of claustrophobia. Not exactly a good thing, because without that sense of being closed in and unable to get away, that switch inside she'd flicked earlier, unswitched. Yvaine looked around at the mass of monsters that hadn't yet seen them and tried to hold on to the panic that was integral to her weird power. Until they moved in to capture her again the ability would fade.

Stupid. She really should have worked on honing her skill a little bit instead of only relying on it during fight or flight situations. Now they needed a new whole new plan. "I will tell you right now we are not jumping off this roof, or climbing down the side of the building, or--"

Jett's eyes turned to fire like the beasts around her. A black shimmer skated across his skin and she got the distinct impression of teeth and claws and scales trying to burst forth.

Poopapalooza.

Was he one of them and had tricked her? Was that even a thing? Men who were also beasts? Only if this was a flipping fairy tale. Which it was not. Man, she hoped she was hallucinating. Or drunk. Yes, drunk would be good right about now.

He dropped her hand and Yvaine gasped as it transformed into dark black skin and sharp scary looking talons extended. Double poo. She backed away, not like she knew where she was going but she couldn't take her eyes off of him as his body continued to morph. He stretched his neck and a row of black spikes erupted along his spine, and then great big wings burst forth. She was in so, so, so much deep, stinky poo. Like up poop creek and not only did she not have a paddle, she didn't even have a canoe.

The necklace around her throat glowed with an eerie black and red light and sparks that matched the shimmer drifting over the creature Jett was becoming. In another blink, the man was gone and a full on mean-ass black dragon roared like an oncoming freight train filled with freight trains.

Yvaine sank to her knees and covered her ears at the blast of sound. The batstriches around her turned to Jett and some returned his call with bellows of their own and others jumped around spitting fire and flapping their wings, which were weenie next to Jett's expansive span. The creature, the dragon he'd become resembled the monsters in the way a killer whale resembled a clown fish. There were similarities, but there was no comparison.

The Jett dragon flapped his wings and lifted into the air. He snatched for her with his claws but missed. Yvaine didn't remember moving three feet to the left.

Hold still, Yvaine.

Ack. He was inside her mind. "Stay away, you monster."

I'm trying to save you, dammit.

"Get out of my head. I will, uh, resist your mind control." She mentally threw up brick walls covered in concrete and barbed wire in her thoughts.

The dragon rolled its big black eyes. She didn't realize magical beasts could do that. Wait, what was she saying? She didn't even know dragons or batstriches existed at all. It certainly didn't matter what kind of sarcastic facial expressions they could or could not make. Especially when they were about to kidnap and eat her.

I'm not controlling your mind. Now get over here so I can grab you and fly us the fuck out of this clusterfucking fuck. Jett blew a strip of fire well past her that sent the nearest batstriches running to avoid the flames. A new wave of them burst from the door leading to the roof and they were closing in on her fast. Crud. If they were after Jett why were they aiming their beady little fire eyes at her now?

She backed toward the flames, but damn they were hot. She'd be lucky if her favorite Deadpool riding a unicorn shirt wasn't singed. Jett was so buying her a new one if it got ruined.

Duck, Yvaine. Now.

Instinct had her dropping to the deck and even with her eyes closed tight she knew he was shooting a new burst of flames at the monsters coming at her. When she got the courage to peek, one eye open she was surrounded with the fire. Everywhere she looked flames were licking up into the sky from the rooftop.

Oh no. Oh no. Oh. No. He'd surrounded her in a ring of fire. And now she had that song stuck in her head. For the second time in as many minutes she was trapped. Which meant she could use her Houdini-ism and get away. Except invisibility wasn't going to keep her from getting burned to a Kentucky fried crisp.

Panic clawed at her skin from the inside out, fear peeled off what little bits of courage she had left in debilitating layers. Dog gone it. Now she really was the damsel in distress and in need of rescuing. As soon as the thought that she couldn't get out on her own and she was in serious danger something really weird happened. She didn't move, she didn't flip her internal switch, she barely even took a breath, but one second she was in the circle of flames closing in on her, and the next she wasn't.

Yvaine. Yvaine, where are you? Answer me, dammit.

She looked to the left, then to the right. Both ways all she saw was wide open sky with more rooftops all around. "I don't know."

She spun around and saw the batstriches, the fire, and Jett flying above them about a hundred yards away on the next building over. Huh. One more mark in the ways she was a mutant checklist. She had no idea of she'd been transported ala Star Trek, run across the rooftop super-fast like the Flash, or now had the ability to apparate like Harry Potter.

Those all sounded better than she was actually shit-faced drunk or completely cray-cray. Again, something to think about later. Now was not the time to squander the chance to get away from the fray. This roof didn't have the same access door as the other one. Of course it couldn't be easy. Yvaine searched the area for anyway to get back inside the building. Over on one ledge the metal curves of a ladder down the side clung to some crumbling a stone.

No way. There had to be a trap door or something.

Except there wasn't. The only other structure on the whole roof was some sort of ventilation shaft and there was no way her butt was fitting through those slats. Okay, then. Over the side of the roof it was. But she was going to be really pissed if she fell and died. She would haunt the shit out of the building inspectors.

She peeked over the side to see where the ladder went and came this close to hurling last night's dinner down to the street really, really far below. Holy crow, she hated heights. The metal of the ladder was scorching hot under her hands and the whole structure shook with the slightest movement. Great. She tentatively placed one foot on the top rung. It held.

The faster she got this over with, the faster it would be over. Yvaine very carefully turned her body so she was facing the building and could grip the rungs with both hands. One step, two, three. Only four billion and seven more to go.

She took a breath to steady herself, but that didn't work even a little bit because she wasn't the one shaking. The building was. Only three rungs down the ladder, she could still see over the top and what she saw sucked balls. The batstriches had found her and were jumping from their roof to hers. There was no dragon's fire to protect her this time. All of the flames Jett had blown were surrounding a blank bit of roof on the opposite side of the building. Not useful at all.

Hold on. I'm coming to get you.

The clouds that had darkened the sky overhead went completely black, like a thick smoke, casting a dark shadow over the entire city. Two of the monsters bounded toward her flapping their wings, and another one sprung up in the nearest corner of the roof. All three had her directly in their sights and the closest one spit shots of fire at her. Hey, weren't they supposed to be after Jett and not her?

She needed to get out of here right now. People in the movies went down ladders all fast by placing their hands and feet along the outside of the rails and sliding down like a fireman. She gripped the sides, one in each fist, and then put one foot along the outside edge. A dozen more batstriches jumped from the burning rooftop to hers and the building shook again. Yvaine's heart just about fell out of her chest and down the five stories to the street below. Her arms hugged the ladder of their own accord, her body taking over since her brain was obviously not doing a good job of keeping them safe.

She only needed to slide the ten feet to the next landing and then she could climb back inside the building. She could do that. She absolutely could. As soon as she swallowed the giant knot of fear in her throat. Yep. Okay. Ready? No. Go anyway. She closed her eyes, huffed out a quick breath and moved her hands and feet to the outside of the railing.

She slid past one rung, her foot snagged on some sort of bump in the metal, causing that foot to twist at a hard right angle. Her leg shot out into the air throwing her entire body off balance. The rungs of the ladder were butter through her fingers and in an instant her life was flashing before her eyes along with the side of the building.

Yvaine was going to die. Right here right now. Why hadn't she been a little more naughty in her life? Only the good die young. She screamed the only thing her scared mind could come up with that might possibly save her at this dire moment.

It wasn't for help, it wasn't a prayer, it wasn't even for ice cream. She just screamed for her life. "Jett!"

POOF THE MAGIC DRAGON

*T*hat marked one kind of being off Jett's list of what kind of supernatural being Yvaine might be. Anything with wings was definitely out. If he had to guess right this second, he'd say she was some kind of stone fairy, because she was falling like a rock. Jett tucked in his wings and dove for the ground hoping to grab her before she splatted all over the street.

Hold on. I'm coming for you.

"Hold on to what? Thin air? Help me." Her voice was tinged with real fear and the sound of it grated on Jett's psyche. He did not like that she was scared. Dammit. He'd been less than a meter away from nabbing her off that ladder when one of his brethren had reached out of a shadow on the wall and grabbed her foot. Little fuckers. Couldn't they see he was doing everything in his power not to hurt them?

Of course they could. That's why they were after the girl. They were using her as bait. But who had made that split-second decision? The cursed? Or was the Black Dragon calling the shots? Jett knew his father was close, but hadn't yet made an appearance. They yellow-bellied lizard had sent every minion of hell to this tiny German town.

If he didn't lead them away, Glückstadt would be demolished. He should have already fucking left. But no. He decided to screw around finding a piece of ass. Then saving her ass. Dumb ass. What the hell had he signed up for with this chick? He was invested now.

Yvaine screamed out his name again and the sound went straight down his spine. She couldn't see him yet. The demon dragons were manifesting and smoking up the place. She probably thought he was trying to kill her too. What kind of paranormal being hadn't seen a dragon before?

One millimeter before she hit the cobblestones he snatched her out of the air, wrapping his talons around her and swooping down the street hugging the shadows. He stayed low to the ground using the darkness to hide them just long enough to get out of sight and then took a sharp turn straight up into the sky. Someone else would have to deal with the fall out of the people here seeing a dragon flapping its wings over the town.

"What the chuck, dude? My life was flashing in front of my eyes. I thought you were going to let me die." Her shout was shaky and her body trembled in his claws.

Of course not.

Yvaine clung tightly to his leg and he liked the feeling of her grip on him. If he was smart he'd drop her somewhere outside of town or even better, just drop her right into the water. Except she'd probably freeze to death. Why did he even fucking care if she died? He shouldn't be caring about anything but finding the cure for his brethren's curse so they could escape the clutches of the Black Dragon.

But what fun would that be, my recalcitrant son? The Black Dragon rose up into the sky directly in Jett's flight path.

Holy fuckballs.

Jett closed his talon's tight around Yvaine and twisted, turning in as tight a spiral as he could to avoid colliding with the Black Dragon's wings. The bastard didn't make that easy. He flapped his wings together and blew a hot stream of fire creating a vortex of flames that were coming straight for them.

Neat trick. He'd have to remember that one. But Jett had been avoiding his father's punishments for hundreds of years. This one wasn't going to catch him off guard. He may not be as big as the Black Dragon, but he was much smarter. What he needed was a god-damned blue dragon to put out the flames. Since he didn't have that, he headed straight for the river. There may not be a blue dragon around, but he knew for a fact there were mermen.

"Holy forking shirt. Who was that? Like the king dragon or something. He was flipping huge."

Good guess. You're close. That was the King of Hell.

He'd leave the part out about it also being his father.

"Like the devil? Satan is a dragon?"

No.

Her questions were distracting him and their chances of surviving were already low. He had to get to that river before the flame tornado caught up to them. Jett wasn't going in the drink if he could help it. But Yvaine was. The mers wouldn't let her drown or freeze to death. Once he dropped her off he could turn and fight the Black Dragon without having to worry about keeping her safe. They'd have to fly across half of Glückstadt to get there and the demon dragons were already stalking them.

They were popping up out of the shadows as fast as he could fly past them. They wouldn't go in the water though. It was their kryptonite. Unless of course Ereshkigal, the Black Witch and his father's cohort, had bespelled them for that specific purpose.

Fuck a duck. He was going to have to take that chance. The water made him half useless in his dragon form, and it wasn't like dear old dad took him to swimming lessons in his human form.

Just a little farther. Almost there. A ball of fire shot over his head, missing them by a scale and crashed into a parking lot. His father was being awfully reckless revealing himself and the forces of hell to the humans this way. That had Jett chuckling inside. Desperate much, dad?

It filled him with all kinds of delightful glee to see the Black Dragon freaking the fuck out, but he didn't understand why or what had sent him off. Jett had been free from hell's grip for a while now and it hadn't seemed to matter one fuck. Someone must have betrayed his plan to free the cursed.

By someone he meant Geshtianna, the succubus queen. Bitch was playing both sides. He should have fucking learned his lesson not to trust her. He needed a Trust No One tattoo on his god damned forehead. Item number four hundred and three on his to do list.

The demon dragons were piling up below them in a title wave of black scaly bodies. Jett glanced down at them and then to the water's edge. Damn it all to hell. They were building a wall of themselves to block his path. At the rate their bodies were building up they'd be a barricade he wouldn't get through unharmed before reaching the river.

"Jett, that king dragon just made another flaming wind tunnel on your six. Uh-oh and another one on your three and your nine."

Great. Ass clowns to the left, jokers to the right and they were stuck in the middle. They weren't going north, south, east, or west. Their only choices remaining were up or down. Up meant fighting the Black Dragon. Down meant eating dirt. Two shitty ass choices.

Up or down?

"You're asking me? Don't you have a plan? I thought you had a plan." Yvaine slapped at Jett's leg. "Why don't I actually get to be the damsel in distress? I'm tired of saving your butt today. You owe me, Jett. Down. There."

She was going to save him. Yeah. Right. She did have some fancy pants powers that he didn't yet understand but that had gotten them out of a tight spot. If she was ready to use them again, he was in. Live today and fight the Black Dragon when he was ready to free his brethren. Then they could all defeat the bastard together.

He saw where Yvaine pointed, and it looked like the worst place on the face of the planet to land. A petrol station. In a firepocalypse. Yeah. Great idea. They were so going to die. He shook his head, then spun and tucked his wings, going straight for the shiny black Porsche Boxster parked at the pump. If he was going to die, he might as well do it in a high-performance piece of German automobile engineering. He dropped Yvaine directly into the passenger seat of the convertible and shifted so he was sitting beside her.

The probable owner of the car and the station attendant standing next to it with the gas nozzle in his hand were smart and ran away screaming. Now to hot wire the car. He reached under the console to pop it off. Yvaine reached over, pushed the button on the dash starting the car, threw it into gear, and pushed down on his thigh. His leg jerked in response and he slammed his foot on the gas. The car took off and Jett grabbed the steering wheel, swerving to avoid oncoming traffic.

Yvaine didn't take her hand off his thigh. No, she squeezed it. Hard. "Tell me you think we are well and truly trapped right now."

"I think we are completely fucking dead. Ten more seconds and those flames will reach the petrol tanks and this place will go up in more flames than are in hell. Which is exactly how the demon dragons and their king like it. We're not just trapped, we're fucked, and not in the fun way."

"Okay." Yvaine gripped his leg in the same way she had when he'd been in dragon form. That same sense of enjoyment from her touch shimmered through him. Only the magic he used to shift between forms could compare to the zings she sent through his body. What the hell was this woman and what had she done to him?

"Then hold on." She closed her eyes, scrunched up her nose in the most adorable way, and held her breath.

Before Jett could ask, the fire, the demon dragons, the Black Dragon, and the whole damn town disappeared. Instead of steering the car through the blackened streets of Glück-stadt they transported into a field of wildflowers with the river adjacent. The Boxster bumped and careened, then hit a small mound of dirt. They went flying into the air, Dukes of Hazard style, and landed hard. Jett spun the steering wheel and the only reason they didn't flip and roll the little car was because of the big ass tree they collided with. The car came to an abrupt stop, the airbags exploded in their faces and the world around them went silent in the aftermath.

Jett shook his head to get his wits back about him and speared the airbag with a talon, slowly letting it deflate. Then he did the same to Yvaine's. Her head was resting against it as if it was a pillow. It was decidedly not. He could already see the bruises forming around her nose and eyes from the impact. He was going to be real pissed off if they'd escaped only for her to die in a god-damned car crash.

He pressed his fingers gently against her neck and blew out a shuttered breath when she groaned. She didn't open her eyes but asked, "Are we dead yet?"

"No. Your spell saved us. Again. I've never seen a witch who can do what you can. What are you?"

Yvaine sat back against the seat and tugged down the shirt she was wearing until her soft peachy flesh was covered by a cartoon drawing of a unicorn. "Tired is what I am. If hanging out with you is going to be this exhausting, I'm going to need way more caffeine in my life."

Hanging out. That was not something he'd ever done. Ever. He hunted. He fought. He fucked. He didn't hang. So why did that sound like something he wanted to do with her? Jett reached over and touched her face, very carefully stroking one finger along her cheekbone. "Is that what we've been doing?"

She covered his hand with hers and leaned into the caress. The necklace she wore glowed with a strange black light. "Ow."

No way he was removing his hand. "Sorry. Can you shift and heal yourself?"

"Umm. I don't know what that means. I think there are a lot of things you're going to have to explain to me."

"Your true form. You're not a witch. Are you not a shifter either? I've imagined you as a cute chubby-cheeked bunny rabbit more than once today." One that he'd like to eat right up.

Her eyes went wide and she slapped his hand away. "Did you just call me chubby?"

"Whoa, whoa, whoa. Don't get mad. I happen to like--"

"Oh man. You're trying to pretend you're a chubby chaser, aren't you?" She pulled at the door handle, but the metal was crumpled and didn't budge. Even slamming her shoulder against it didn't get the door open. She growled at the door in a very cute and sexy way and then climbed up on her seat and slid over the side of the car. "How many mythical creatures am I going to come across today? A dragon I could almost believe, but a hot dude who likes my curves. Yeah, right."

She put air quotes around the word curves and then stomped off across the field. Jett couldn't hear what all she was muttering, partly because he was mesmerized by the sway of her hips and the way she kept throwing her arms up in the air in all kinds of gesticulations. Damn she was even more adorable when she was mad.

He glanced around the field to make sure there were no demon dragons popping up out of the shadows and that they were safe for the time being. Nada. Good. Because no doubt about it. Whether this girl thought she was hot or not, he was definitely going to fuck her until she was screaming out his name over and over. He'd show her exactly how tantalizing her body was to him. Those hips he could grip hard while he was driving his cock into her, those thighs he was going to use for earmuffs, and the ass he was going to spend hours worshipping with his tongue.

Jett hopped out of the steaming pile of Porsche and stalked Yvaine across the field. She was still muttering to herself when he tossed her over his shoulder.

"Hey, what are you doing, you ash face? Put me down,

right now." She pounded against his back and tried to kick her legs, but all that did was wiggle her ass under his arm.

Not a chance, little bunny. It wasn't like he was going to fuck her right here and now. He wanted something more from her than simply great sex. He wanted it to mean something.

What the fuck was he thinking? No, he didn't want that. He would never mean anything to anyone. He had one goal in life and that was to free his brethren and kill the Black Dragon. That was it. Nothing more, nothing less. What did he think? That he was going to mark her, claim her? That she was going to be his mate or some shit?

He did not have what the Dragon warriors he had. He was the bastard son of the king of hell. Love was not something he would ever have in his life and he needed to pull his head out of his ass right this second and forget he'd ever met this beautiful, lush, sensuous woman that made him feel more alive than he ever had in his hundreds of years of existence.

His growl rumbled low in his belly. His head screamed at him to set her down, fly the fuck away from here. Now. Fly away. Right now. He couldn't do it.

"Uhh, you're setting the field on fire."

What?

Jett set Yvaine down and batted at the grass under his feet. He's been so damn far inside his own ass he hadn't even noticed he'd been spewing fire. He'd singed a black path of burnt grass and earth marking his every step. He was lucky the entire field hadn't gone up in flames. That wouldn't be a literal smoke signal to the Black Dragon to come and find them or anything.

Jett ran a hand through his hair and stared at Yvaine. "Release me from your spell, witch, or fairy, or nymph, or whatever the hell you are. These thoughts and feelings you've put into me are going to get us killed."

"I didn't do anything. You're the one who turned into a dragon and carried me away. It's not my fault you lit everything on fire."

Turned into a dragon? "You must have bumped your head harder than I thought. I'm in my human form."

He waved his hand up and down his body to punctuate the 'duh' in his tone.

"You are now. But you weren't when you picked me up. One second you're calling me names and poof, the next second you're Puff the Magic Dragon."

"That is not how shifting magic works. I have to consciously change my form. It doesn't happen by accident."

"Are you sure?"

Yes.

"Well, then I think your shifter is broken, because you're a dragon again."

Jett glanced down at his hands, but they weren't there. His scaly talons and claws were. *What are you doing to me? How are you controlling my dragon?*

He flapped his wings and lifted up into the air. If she had the power to control his shift she was very bad news. Even Ereshkigal, the Black witch didn't have that power. Maybe she was the fabled White Witch the Dragon warriors were all on about. She was supposedly the one who'd given all of dragon kind the ability to shift in the first place.

If she was, he needed to stay. The White Witch was also the mythical being who'd given the dragons the ability to find their mates. They all got a soul shard, given to them by the white witch when they came of age. It contained a small piece of their souls intertwined with that of the First Dragon. When they were in the presence of their mates, it glowed and told them who she was.

Jett had once thought that if he could possess a soul shard he could find a mate of his own. A woman who would complete his soul. He thought she would be the key to breaking the curse.

He'd been wrong.

EENIE MEENIE MINEY MOE, CATCH A DRAGON BY THE TOE

*D*ragons. What the duck, man? One second he was a hot guy, the next he was a fire-breathing monster. Which somehow was Yvaine's fault. Yeah, no.

"Whatever dark spell you're weaving, stop it, now. If you were sent by Ereshkigal or Geshtianna you can go straight back to them and then to hell. I will not be captured or fooled by either of them again."

A minute ago she'd thought he was dragging her off to the bushes to have some sort of make-out session. A minute before that he'd been concerned about her well-being after their car had crashed. She could kind of see why he thought she was the one doing a magic trick on him. She had super duper transported them out of the battle in Glückstadt and out here to the middle of nowhere. That had never happened before. None of this was even a part of her abnormal normal.

This was not her ducking fault. She stomped her foot. This was the last thing she needed. "I'm not doing anything."

Black light, red sparkles and poof. Once again man became dragon.

Obviously you are. His tail swished in the grass behind him and caught a gopher or a squirrel or something, flipping the poor thing up in the air and into a nearby tree. Jett spun in a circle like a puppy surprised by his own tail and then narrowed those big dark dragon eyes on Yvaine again. *God dammit. At least leave me in one form or the other for a half a fucking minute.*

Smoke poured out of his nostrils and Yvaine did not relish getting lit on fire. He was pissed. A tiny voice in the back of her mind told her his anger wasn't entirely directed at her. She'd hoped it was right, because she was about to get real with him. She spread her hands out in a placating gesture and instead of stepping away like she should, she moved toward him.

"Look. I don't know what's going on with you. I didn't even know dragons existed until like a half an hour ago. But I do get that you're scared and frustrated." She could relate. His body was seemingly out of his control and he didn't know what to do about it. Samesies.

I'm not scared. He huffed even though the words were in her head and not out of his shiny black snout.

If she didn't know better...and she really didn't... she'd think that was a dragon pouty face.

"I would be. I have been. That, that," She waved her hand toward the crumpled car. "I don't know what, dissapparation, I guess, we did back there? I think I did that, but I don't know how or why. You obviously think I'm a witch or something else out of a fairy tale, but I don't understand what happens when I go all invisible either. That scares the bejeezus out of me."

Jett tilted his head to the side, again reminding her of a curious puppy. One she'd like to snuggle up with. Except of course when he looked like he was going to gobble her up in one bite. She took a couple of steps back from that intense glare he had pointed at her.

He sat down on his haunches and scratched at the ground. *I can't tell if you are lying to me. Your scent doesn't betray you, but only a white witch has powers like yours. I know another who did not know the depth of her powers either. Although she is sweet and doesn't pick people's pockets.*

Sigh. Of course she doesn't. She was probably a beautiful, thin, tall, blonde with great boobs and more money than she knew what to do with too. "Yeah, well, I'm sure she's flippin' lovely."

Jett sniffed the air, brought his head down closer to her and snuffled right between her shoulder and her ear sending zings of shivers all through her body. He took one long inhale and sat back, looking proud of himself for invading her personal space with his snout. *You're jealous.*

"What? No. Why would I be jealous?" She threw her arms in the air and turned her back on him. Jealous. Of what? Pshaw. Nothing. She had nothing to be jealous of.

He bumped her shoulder with his tail trying to get her to turn back around. Poof. "But you are."

Why, oh why did his voice have to send all the tingles to her girly parts? It wasn't fair. She was trying to distance herself from him. He was a crazy ass dragon man she was absolutely not going to continue to be attracted to. "I cannot scent your lies, but your jealousy, and now embarrassment are coming off you like a sweet piece of candy. One I enjoy very much. That I'd like to eat."

Don't turn around, don't turn around. He was just trying to bait her. She knew better. There had been plenty of boys at the convent's orphanage who loved to tease and torment her.

Granted none of them had been a shape-shifting dragon. Instead of playing his game, Yvaine started walking back toward the car. She didn't have her few meager things anymore, her bag was somewhere in a mass of batstriches back in Glückstadt. If she was lucky, the unfortunate owner of the car was on vacation and there would be a suitcase full of plus-sized women's clothes and a mobile phone with hundreds of pre-paid minutes somewhere in the wreckage.

"Yvaine," he growled her name in a way that was more a caress, than a warning. "Where do you think you're going?"

She increased her pace and did not look over her shoulder. She didn't bother being careful of where she stepped even though she should pick her way through the possible mine-field of wildlife holes, rocks, twigs, and other things that could trip her up. "We should probably go our separate ways now that we're out of danger. Since I can't fly away from here I call dibs on whatever's in the car."

In a blink Jett was standing in front of her, blocking her way. "Oh no you don't. Not while you can control my shape. I'm not letting you out of my sight."

"I told you I'm not doing anything." Yvaine brushed against his muscled arm and sidestepped him without even stopping. The faster she ransacked the car the sooner she could get out of there. She had enough of dragons for one lifetime. An angry squirrel popped up out of the car scaring her half to death. Probably the partner of the one that had gone flying up into the tree earlier.

A big black dragon butt landed right on top of the car, squishing it into the dirt and sending the squirrel scampering. *You are whether you know how you are doing it or not. You're stuck with me until we can figure out how to make it stop.*

Gah. She had places to go, people to see. Family to find.

Maybe they could explain what was going on with her and her dragon. She'd probably get to her birthplace sooner on the back of a dragon than hitchhiking. Not that she'd even consider riding on his back. "I wish you would stop doing that. Talking into my head, I mean. Can you hear my thoughts?"

No. As far as I know only dragons can communicate with each other with mind speak. He scratched at a spot on his chest. *Or with their mates.*

That word, mates, stopped Yvaine in her tracks. "Exsqueeze me?"

Don't worry, babe. I don't get a mate. Ever.

An intense denial hit her in the stomach like a bad veggie burrito. "What do you mean by mate? Like a BFF? You're making it sound like dragons are from down under, but you don't sound Australian. Wait. Why don't you get to have friends?"

Mate. As in soul mate. One true love. The one being in the universe who is the match for your true self.

"Oh." Ohhhhh. Well that plucking sucked. Yvaine may not know anything about soul mates, but she wanted to believe there was someone out there for everyone. Even weirdos like her and Jett deserved love.

"But you don't get one. Sounds like bullshirt to me, beetee dubs. But I can hear you." Why was she arguing with him? He deserved to have a woman or a dragon woman in his life. But she wasn't it. She didn't want to be his soul mate. Yvaine smacked her tongue inside of her mouth a few times. A sour taste swirled in the back of her throat.

You must have dragon blood in you.

"Is that a thing? Like people walking around not knowing they are the descendants of dragons? Um, eww. Like did a dragon god have sex with a human as some point in history? Come to think of it, I do know some nuns who definitely seem like they could breathe fire, so maybe."

As far as I know, there are no other female dragons or even female dragon descendants. But it is the only explanation I can come up with. He looked everywhere but at her.

Yvaine had no idea who her parents were and by the sound of it she may not even know what they were. She rubbed her forehead. "I'm having a real hard time believing I'm anything other than a slightly weird human."

You're anything but human. That was obvious to me the second you walked into the pub last night. Where are your people? Why didn't they teach you about your abilities?

Ouch. Sore point. "Maybe they didn't know either."

They wouldn't have left her if they had. She wouldn't have grown up thinking she was nothing more than a freak.

Then let's go to them now and I will force them to teach you how to use your abilities. Where are they?

Now it was Yvaine's turn to look anywhere but at him and scratch around in the dirt with the toe of her shoe. She shrugged and chewed on the inside of her cheek.

I see. The snout of the dragon snuffled her in the throat again which was stupidly comforting. The glow from the necklace she was wearing lit up and little sparks floated around in the air between them. Jett's form shifted again and in place of a snout his lips were against her skin. Cheeze-whiz that felt good.

"What a pair of lost souls we are, you and I. Maybe that's why I have this debilitating attraction to you." He kissed her collarbone and then scraped his teeth across her skin.

Yvaine's knees almost gave out when he did that. "Oh, gosh. Do that again."

"This?" He nibbled on her ear and sucked it into his mouth. His hands wandered south, one settling into the small of her back and the other cupping her butt cheek.

Normally she didn't let anyone touch her bum. She had always been too self-conscious about the size. She leaned into Jett's touch. "No. The other thing. Although that's nice too and you could go back to that later."

"Ah. You mean this." He squeezed her butt and pulled her closer, grinding his pelvis against hers.

Whoa. Either there was dragon in his pocket or he was very happy to see her. "Stop teasing me. Do the thing with my neck. Please."

"Mmm," he growled and Yvaine felt the rumbles all the way to her core and between her legs. "I like hearing you beg me. Do it again and maybe I'll give you what you want."

That was enough of that. She speared her hands into his hair and pulled him down to the sensitive skin that was really doing the begging for him. No one had ever said that space between her shoulder and her neck was so sensitive. "Do it, Jett."

He licked that spot and drug his teeth over her skin again. They both moaned and the world around them filled up with black light and red sparks. Or maybe those were just behind her eyelids. She couldn't seem to keep them open for all the intensity of the kisses he was giving to her. He nipped at her skin with his teeth and she wanted nothing more than for him to bite her.

She'd never wanted anyone to do that to her. She'd wanted plenty of boys to kiss her. Not that very many had. Consequences of living at a convent with nuns. Biting hadn't even been in her fantasies. She definitely wanted Jett to use his teeth on her. She gripped his hair tighter and glued her body to his.

He breathed her in and moaned her name. "Yvaine. What are you doing to me? Why can't I control anything about myself around you?"

She didn't get a chance to answer because a huge explosion shook the ground. Together they stared at the burst of flames and dark black smoke spewing into the air no less than a mile away. A wave of heat and percussion smacked into them and Jett's dragon form flickered to the surface before he tackled her to the ground covering her body with his.

For about the four-thousandth time today adrenaline shot through her. Very much more of this and she was going to run out of the stuff. Although, it was just as rapidly being replaced with whatever hormones had her girly parts excited about being squished under Jett. She took several shuttered breaths which didn't help even a little bit since her nose was all filled up with the smoky sexy as sin scent of him. That must be a new version of Axe body spray. L'eau de Draekon. Mmm. Oh, cripes, she needed to get her head and those excited girl bits to quit it. "Do you think that was the petrol station?"

Jett stared down at her and his eyes were smiling like he knew everything that had been going through her head. "Yeah. We're not as far from the town as I'd hoped we were. We need to get out of here."

"Uh-huh." Was that her voice that sounded all Marylin Monroe-ish?

"Probably." He didn't move. His eyes did though. Down to her mouth and back up again.

Had all the air suddenly gone from this big wide-open field? Or maybe she'd forgotten how to breathe. She did manage to croak out, "yeah, probably."

Jett looked disappointed and rolled off of her. Yvaine felt really dumb for missing the heat and weight of him over her. It was for the best because she had totally been ready to get it on with him right here in the middle of a field. That had to be the left over adrenaline talking. That was a thing, she was sure of it. It was in movies anyway.

He reached down and grabbed her hand, pulling her back up. Without releasing her fingers from his, he led her back toward the car wreckage. "Change me back into my dragon form and I will fly us somewhere safe."

"Umm." She was starting to believe that maybe she had some other powers besides her Houdini-ism, but she sure as shirt didn't know how to use them on purpose. Besides. She didn't want to fly anywhere. She preferred two feet on the ground at all times, thank you very much.

Jett rolled his eyes. "You're going to tell me you're not doing it, aren't you?"

"Even if I am, I don't know how. Can't we just walk? I like walking. Or how about the train. Europe has great rails." She was just about to expound upon the benefits of a Eurail pass and how they could go pretty much anywhere when a second explosion sounded from the town. This one wasn't as strong as the last, and all they did was duck a little. Like that was going to do anything. At least her heart wasn't beating out of her chest this time.

"Turn around, I have a theory." He spun her so she was facing the car with him behind her.

Yvaine brushed the dirt off her jeans and picked the grass out of the unicorn's mouth on her t-shirt where it had gotten mashed in. That was going to stain. It had been a long time since she'd had new clothes like these ones. She hated to have them ruined. Maybe they could stop into a shop when they got to the next town. The train station would definitely have something touristy she could buy...with Jett's money in her pocket. "What's your idea?"

Jett smacked her ass hard and shouted in her ear. "Spider."

Yvaine jumped at least a foot and almost fell into the wreckage. "Ack. What the H E double hockey-sticks, Jett?"

Interesting.

Yvaine grabbed her throat and took a long breath to get her heart to slow back down. "Your theory was if you scared the hiccups out of me you'd shift back into a dragon?"

Yes, and it worked. Now get back in the car. We need to leave this area before the Black Dragon figures out where we are.

He was so deadpan that Yvaine had to laugh. "What? No. It's literally a wreck if you hadn't noticed."

I did. If I touch you, that also triggers your magic and I'll turn back into a human. I can't fly us out of here if I do. He pushed the car away from the tree and then dipped his head indicating she should get in the freed car.

Huh. She wasn't convinced. "But nothing happened when I kissed you last night. Or when you were dragging me through the batstriches back there in the town. So how do you figure?"

You weren't wearing that magic necklace last night.

Yvaine put her hand over the charm hanging from her neck. It sat so comfortably in the center of her chest, she could hardly remember a time when it hadn't been there. It was so much a part of her she could feel it in her soul. So why couldn't she remember where or even when she'd gotten it? But Jett was right. She must have taken it off. Strange.

Dark clouds rolled through the smoke from the petrol station explosion and the sky darkened. Uh-oh. That did not look good. She inched slightly closer to the car with all its jagged metal edges. Crapballs, she did not want to get in there nor did she want Jett to pick her up with it and fly away. What if she fainted? What if he dropped her? What if an airplane collided with them and everyone died but the aviation disaster inspectors couldn't figure out why there was a Porsche, a dinosaur, and an extra weird girl in the wreckage along with the passengers and the black box?

Gulp. That building they'd been on top of was the highest she'd ever been off the ground. They should have started walking instead of half making out in that field. Maybe she should start running.

We need to go, now. Get in. Jett spit a tiny burst of flames near her feet, not close enough to actually burn her, but she moved away to avoid it anyway.

"Hey. Keep your fire to yourself there, mister. I'm going already. But what if we--"

Get in the god-damned car. We've got about seven seconds before demon dragons start showing up in those shadows. We escaped once, but the Black Dragon is not stupid and he will not let us evade him again.

"Jett comes now."

Yvaine heard the beast pop up behind her. His hot breath curled the hair on the back of her neck, and the claw that speared through her back that came out through the front of her chest smelled like a combination of rotting hamburger and cotton candy.

Mmm. Cotton candy.

That was the last thing that went through her mind before the world went all rainbows and sparkles.

IN WHICH JETT BECOMES A DOUCHEPOTATO

*E*ven though he was in dragon form with his tough armored scales, and nothing had touched him, a pain so intense and overwhelming hit him directly in the heart. He pitched to the side and fell onto the shattered hood of the car.

Yvaine.

His vision blurred and he had to fight for consciousness. He could not let his cursed brother take him to hell and leave Yvaine all alone here to die. Her head lolled to the side but he couldn't see any blood. A slimy silvery substance like pure mercury coated the claw of the demon dragon who'd speared her through the heart.

The demon dragon was trembling, not from fear, but almost like a seizure. Jett doubted now that she was any sort of a dragon. He hoped whatever Yvaine was, her blood was lethal. None of the cursed would die by his hand, but he wished death upon this particular brother of his. Which appeared imminent if the way his eyes were rolling back in his head and the silvery froth foamed at his mouth.

Jett struggled to his feet and kicked the demon dragon

away. Its claw made a horrifying slurpy sucking sound as it pulled back out of Yvaine's chest. The silver continued to flow out of the wound and pooled on the ground. He didn't dare touch it or Yvaine. If he were to shift into his weaker human form now there would be no saving either of them. If she was even still alive.

The tiniest moan passed through her lips, so quiet he wasn't even sure he'd heard it or imagined it. But his vision cleared and some of his strength seeped back into his muscles. The necklace at her chest flickered and the black light it emitted swirled around the wound, its red sparks crawling inside of her. Jett shook his head to make sure what he was seeing was real.

Son, get your ass up. This is no time to be lazing around. The voice of another dragon sounded in his head. It wasn't his father, though. This male was older, kinder in his demands. *I can't risk showing myself with Jara so near. It would spoil the element of surprise. So this is all you're going to get of me.*

Who are you? Jett pushed up and tested his wings to see if he could spread them, use them to get out of there.

We'll save that discussion for another day. For the time being you only need to know that we're on your side. Now hurry up. The disembodied voice put some sort of power behind his words and Jett found himself fully upright and filled with renewed strength.

He glanced around to see what he could use to lift Yvaine into the car without touching her. The convertible top that had been stowed into the back of the car had sprung free and was partially unfurled. Jett grabbed it in his talons and ripped the metal and material from its housing. He stomped on it being careful not to shred the fabric and it spread nicely into a hammock shape. Screw the car. He'd carry her out of here in this contraption. As soon as he figured out how to get her onto it.

A woman's voice, beautiful and sensual, but scared popped into his head. She was most definitely not talking to him. *Kur, he's coming. I can't see him. I just can't. We must go now.*

Yes, my love. I know. Give the girl a little boost and we'll be gone.

An uncomfortably long silence had Jett worried she wasn't going to help Yvaine. It was on the tip of his tongue to either promise her retribution if she didn't or anything she wanted if she would. Not like he could repay either. Hard to mete out justice or rewards when you had no idea who you were talking to.

Fine. She was so not happy to be here. *But you talk to that boy about what he needs to do so this doesn't happen again. I will not have a douchepotato in my family. Do you hear me?*

Douchepotato? Family? Who was she talking about? Not Jett. Except there was no one else around that the woman could be calling him a feminine hygiene vegetable.

Yes, dear. I'll take care of it.

Jett didn't care who or what these being were, or their agenda in helping him. He couldn't care that they implied that he was family. He only wanted to get Yvaine and get away. The black and red light from the necklace shimmered and became an almost blinding white light. It lifted Yvaine up and her unconscious body gently floated into the center of the make-shift stretcher. Jett didn't waste any time gathering the ends of the contraption and lifting up into the air. He didn't know where he was going, but he knew he needed to get as far away from that field and into the sunlight where the Black Dragon could not see him.

Take her to the Green Dragon Wyvern, son. He will be able to heal her.

Jett didn't think twice about whether that instruction would mean his own certain demise. Okay, maybe he did. The Green Dragon Wyvern and his mate owed him. But dragon warriors were just as likely to betray him as repay any favors. He was only one step removed from their greatest enemy and they didn't trust him.

That was okay, because he didn't trust anyone. He had spent his recent freedom building up a hoard of favors from the Wyverns. They all owed him something except for the Red one. That guy hated his guts even though they'd never even crossed paths. At least Ciara, the Green Wyvern's mate was an ally. Sort of. He'd use that in to get the dragon to heal Yvaine. Maybe she could help explain Yvaine's powers and get them unlinked too.

Jett immediately banked left and pushed his wings hard to gain altitude. The sooner he could get to the outskirts of Prague and the Green Wyvern's villa there the better. Only then and when Yvaine was out of danger would he take the time to think about who it was that was helping them.

She will heal. When she does quit screwing around. The voice faded as if by flying in this direction he was leaving the speaker behind. *Mark her, claim her.* His final words came to him more of a thought than whispered mindspeak. *Make her your mate.*

Jett's wings faltered and he sank about a hundred meters in altitude before he recovered. No. He must have heard that wrong. He couldn't. He didn't have a soul. Without that he couldn't have a mate either.

Mark her.

He hadn't been raised in the dragon warrior culture to

know if that term had a particular significance or if it was simply literal. He'd seen the dragon tattoo-like marks on the mates he'd encountered. Ciara had a sparkling green dragon etched into the skin at her neck. Exactly in the same spot where he'd wanted to bite Yvaine. That need was pure instinct. He obviously couldn't even do that correctly. Ciara's mark was beautiful and had probably been lovingly applied by her dragon mate. Jett's mouth ached to chomp down on the female he was attracted to. God, he was such a... douchepotato.

Why he was even thinking about this, he didn't know. He could probably mark Yvaine, clumsily. He could lay claim to her too. Which would all pretty much ruin her chances of ever finding a real mate. He'd already screwed up another woman's life thinking he could trick the universe. Portia would never forgive him. He'd like to blame his father, the Black Witch, and the Succubus Queen for putting the idea in his head in the first place.

Steal a soul shard they'd said. It'll bring you everything you ever wanted, they'd said. They'd all been wrong. It had only shown him the depth of how completely fucked his empty soulless shell of a life really was. There was no way he was going through all of that again.

The sooner he could be rid of Yvaine and her control over him, the better.

Jett? Her too soft voice pierced right into the blackness of his thoughts. *Are we dead? Is this heaven? It's not very nice if it is. Where are the puppies and rainbows?*

Shh. You were injured. I'm taking you to someone that will heal you. Then hopefully leaving her there. He'd been around her for less than a day and she'd already wreaked so much havoc in his life he didn't know if he was flying up or down or sideways. He'd lost all perspective on what he needed to do the second she walked into that pub last night. If he hadn't gone after her he could be out hunting for the spell dealer he'd been waiting to show up in that stupid town. He'd be one step closer to finding the cure for the curse.

That's nice. Is the healer dead too? Do I need to be healed if I'm dead? She sounded soft and dreamy like she was drugged. What had the mysterious voices done to her?

Why did he care so much? He didn't. If he kept telling himself that he'd eventually believe it. His mindspeak voice came out gruffer then he intended. *You're not dead.*

She was silent for long enough he thought maybe she'd passed out again. Or perhaps his reprimand had hurt her fucking feelings. He pushed his wings harder and searched for a warm air current to help push them toward Prague all the faster.

Are you sure? I think I am. I feel dead. Wait. Does dead hurt? My chest hurts.

Jett mentally breathed a sigh of relief. Hurt meant alive. He could attest to that. *You're alive. I promise.*

Okay. Are we there yet?

Instead of answering her he banked again. They were just over the Volga river which meant they were close. He shouldn't even know where the Green Dragon Wyvern's lair was. He wouldn't if Geshtianna hadn't sent him here when he'd first sought refuge with her. How she had known the Wyvern had met his mate was some pretty shady collusion. Or so he suspected.

Believing Geshtianna was on his side had been his first mistake after escaping hell. Nasty little Queens like her would get her comeuppance. She'd already been chased from her court in Dubai by the dragon warriors. When he was ready to call in the ultimate favor, he'd tell them exactly where she'd taken refuge. He was not above playing both sides to get what he wanted.

Jakob's villa came into view and along with it the shimmering wards to keep him and his kind out. They were much stronger than the last time he'd been here. Must be Ciara's powers. She was a white witch after all. Jett flew in a wide circle over the top of the villa, testing the wards for weaknesses. At his first touch green light flashed through the wards.

Shit. He'd set off some sort of alarm. He didn't even count to three before two really fucking big green dragons were in the air and flanking him. They were much clumsier flyers than he was since their element was earth and he could either outmaneuver them which his dragon screamed at him to do, or let them capture him. That's what he needed to do if he wanted inside those wards. But even the thought of being under any other dragon's control rankled the fuck out of him.

You are in the Green Wyvern's airspace. Drop your weapon and land now.

Jett's knee jerk reply was to tell them to fuck off and shoot a few fireballs over their heads. He couldn't risk them retaliating and harming Yvaine. *It's a woman not a weapon, dumbasses. I'm not dropping her.*

One of the two guards didn't like that answer and flew directly at him forcing him into evasive maneuvers. One giant swoop up and he was loopty-looping over the big asshole's head. He was sure as shit gambling on centripetal force to keep Yvaine in her convertible top stretcher. Jett came in behind the green dragons and sent a warning shot of fire over their heads.

Don't be dicks. Just show me where to land. I mean no one any harm.

Said dicks responded as dickishly as they could. Green vines burst up out of the ground like a fucking bean stalk aiming for his jack-ass. The first one narrowly missed smacking him in the chest and he disintegrated the other with a burst of flames. A third and fourth vine split off from the other, but this time with giant thorns on it. The two dragons careened toward him boxing him in on all sides. The vines aimed straight for his wings and he had nowhere to go to avoid getting captured.

That was going to fucking hurt. More thorny vines sprouted around him so Jett curled in on himself, tucking Yvaine's carrier under him as best he could to protect her from the brunt of the attack. The vines struck, piercing his wings and dragged them toward the ground. Fuck, fuck, fuck. At this angle he'd crush Yvaine under him.

Jett? It feels like pins are pricking me in the arm. What's happening?

Jett pulled in a deep breath. He'd fry every one of these mother fuckers for not listening. Their arrogance was going to get Yvaine killed. The vines wrapped themselves more tightly around him and one of the greens pounced onto his back, pushing him down and crashing through the wards. The blast of magic from the protective barrier shot through him before he could blow the green dragons and their plants out of the sky, knocking all of the wind out of him. He shot toward the ground like a meteor. If he didn't squash her to death under him, the collision would kill her.

Stop. You'll kill her and then I'll have to kill you. Jett twisted his body, trying like hell to get under Yvaine thinking he could maybe absorb some of the impact. The ground was coming up too fast and he only made it just to his side.

Hold on, babe. This is going to be a bumpy landing. Jett closed his eyes tight and hoped for the best.

Just then, the best showed up.

A strong wind grabbed him before they hit the ground and carried them over to a big pile of hay. The golden stalks swirled in the breeze and softened the landing, cradling the two of them. The vines around him shrank and disintegrated into nothing more than blades of grass, releasing his wings. He slid down the haystack and quickly let go of Yvaine's carrier so he didn't roll over her on his way to the ground. She tumbled out and ended up directly on top of him. His form shifted back to human at her touch and he sat up cupping her head in his lap.

He examined her and she looked pale, but was still breathing and alive. He brushed hay and hair away from her face and her eyelashes fluttered open. Those brilliant lavender eyes stared up at him like he was some kind of savior. In that brief moment, he wanted to be that for her.

He couldn't though. Jett had other work to do and the sooner he remembered that and got Yvaine, and her beautiful eyes, lush body, hilarious fashion sense, and her magic, out of his life, the sooner he could get back to breaking the curse and freeing his brethren. Please let him have made the right choice in bringing her to the Green Wyvern. Yvaine breathed out a soft sigh and closed her eyes again.

A second of panic made his heart skip a beat. That wasn't her last breath ever was it? No. Her chest rose and fell and the tiniest bit of color seeped into her cheeks. Thank the First Dragon.

Which was something he'd never even thought, much less

meant ever before. He was going to do something else he hadn't before right now. Ask for help. "Wyvern, Ciara. Yvaine needs your help."

A curvy blonde he'd always had quite the crush on ran over to them and squatted down beside him. "Jett? What are you doing here?"

"Yes, black dragon rogue. What are you doing here?" The alpha voice of Jakob Zeleny rang through Jett. If he'd been a green dragon, he'd be cowering for the Wyvern. Jett bowed to no man or dragon.

"Trying not to let your fucktard guard kill this woman. You need to get those asshole's hearing aids. I told them I wasn't here to harm anyone." Bastards. They definitely needed their dinner poisoned later. Just enough to give them a bad case of the shits.

Jakob didn't look one wit bothered by Jett's reprimand and the two green dragons continued to circle overhead looking smug. "Their duty to protect the Green Wyr stronghold and my mate. Both are very enthusiastic about their jobs."

The ever lovely Ciara rolled her eyes at her mate and kissed him on the cheek. "Tell your dragons good job, Jakey-poo, but maybe they could remember next time that Jett is our ally."

Jakob folded his arms across his chest. "He's not."

"I saved your stupid life and that of your mate's. You owe me, Greenie-poo." Ciara wouldn't even be here if Jett hadn't protected her from the demon dragons. Granted he'd wanted her for his own at the time and certainly hadn't intended it to be helpful to Jakob. No one but Geshtianna knew that. She was the one who'd told him Ciara was a dragon's mate and where to find her. She'd told the Black Dragon the same thing.

"I let you live just now. That repays any debt I have to you."

"Not even close." No way. Jett was counting on calling in those favors when he broke the curse. As much as he hated to admit it. He was going to need the dragon warriors help to defeat his father.

Ciara held out her hands and the tiniest of snowflakes sparkled around her fingers. "Now, gentlemen. Maybe you can get your rulers out and measure later. First let's help Jett's friend into the house where she'll be more comfortable than rolling around in the hay."

There he was being a fucking dumbass again. He'd been ready to up and fist fight Jakob over a few words and Yvaine was lying in his lap probably dying. One more reason, besides the fact that he didn't have a soul, that there was no way he could ever be mated to any woman. He stood and lifted Yvaine into his arms. "Jakob. She is hurt. I was sent here because you can heal her."

Jakob nodded and Ciara indicated that Jett should follow her. The entered the house, and god damn, these Wyverns had a lot of fucking money if the size of the rooms and the fancy furniture and decorations were any indication. He was almost afraid to touch anything for fear of getting it dirty. Except that might be fun. Place needed a little filthying up. It was way too pristine, and shiny, and bright

"Lay her down over here. Has she been able to shift to heal herself at all?" Ciara flicked her hand and a soft cloth floated in from the kitchen.

Jett laid Yvaine on the dark green couch and gently slid a weird little tubular pillow behind her head. "No. She doesn't seem to know what she is. I don't think she was raised in our world or by anyone who knows about the paranormal at all. She mentioned that she didn't know who or where her people were and she doesn't have any idea how her own powers work."

Ciara nodded and then dabbed the cloth at the smears of silver slime that had spattered from Yvaine's wound to her face, neck, and arms. "Welcome to the club then."

Jakob knelt beside Ciara and blew a long stream of green smoke first over Yvaine's face and then again at the wound in her chest. Jett clenched and released his fists. He didn't like Jakob being that close to Yvaine even if he was healing her with his Dragon's breath. He paced back and forth never taking his eyes off Yvaine. He couldn't tell if the stupid Wyvern was healing her or not.

Ciara glanced over at Jett and a cool mist swirled around him. Just like that his anger and frustration, worry and fear, slipped down from the danger zone to a manageable hum in the back of his mind. He raised an eyebrow at Ciara and she smiled back at him. "I've been practicing. Feel better?"

"No," he lied.

"Good." She stuck out her tongue at him and turned back to Yvaine. "The horrible hole in her chest is closing. I don't know how she even survived. What did this to her?"

"Demon dragon." Who was likely a black oil stain in the grass now. Stupid fucker. That was one less soldier Jett would be able to count on in the coming battle against the Black Dragon.

Jakob blew more Dragon's breath over Yvaine. Then he stood and faced Jett. "Were they with Ereshkigal?"

Jett frowned. The Black Witch didn't leave hell and she certainly didn't take demon dragons along with her anywhere. That's what she had her Annunaki demons for. "No. The Black Dragon."

"We haven't seen him since the battle for hell in Africa. We assumed he was licking his wounds, but didn't know where."

"I don't know where he's been, but he found us in Glück-stadt, Germany."

"Not far from The Linden's. Cage will be very interested to hear that. The Golds are still hunting for their kidnapped warriors and Geshtianna." Jakob narrowed his eyes at Jett, waiting for him to reply.

Jett did have intel on Geshtianna's whereabouts and didn't feel even a little bit bad about not telling Jakob that. He was saved once again by Ciara from any more scrutiny from the Green Wyvern who would smell an outright lie if he asked Jett if he knew anything. "She's waking up."

"Holy shirt. What? Who? Ack. Where am I? Jett?"

"Yvaine. I'm here." Holy shirt indeed. She was freaking out and there was no way Jett would be human for more than another-- Poof. *I'm right here.*

"Oops. Sorry."

When she looked up at him with the pink back in her cheeks and the life back in her soul, Jett wasn't even a little bit sorry he'd just smashed every stick of furniture on the side of the room behind his tail.

Ciara looked from Yvaine to Jett and back again. "Well, you could have warned us your mate was going to shift you into dragon form."

She's not my mate.

The laugh that bubbled out of Ciara was contagious apparently because Yvaine and Jakob started laughing too. Ciara laughed so hard tears streamed down her face. She wiped her eyes and gave one more chuckle. "I'm going to have so much fun planning your wedding."

MIMOSAS MAKE EVERYTHING BETTER

A wedding? Surely she hadn't heard that right. Yvaine was not ready to get married to anyone. Oh no. Was the dragon people culture like eighteenth-century England or something? Did they have to get married because they'd kissed? That would be weird. Yvaine was doing a whole lot of assuming here. She didn't know that there even was a dragon culture. So far she'd seen two dragons in her whole entire life. Maybe that's all there was. She didn't know.

Yvaine pushed herself up on the couch and groaned. Man. Ouch. She rubbed her hand over her chest. Did she ever have the worst case of heartburn. She didn't remember eating anything spicy. In fact, the last thing she remembered was Jett trying to convince her to get into the car so they could fly away.

What had happened? They weren't in Kansas anymore. They might just be in the Emerald City though. Every other thing in the room they were in was a shade of green. The couch she was sitting on, the very expensive looking vases on the mantle over the fire place. The big green dragon.

Mother trucker. That was one big dragon. "Whoa. Where did that other dragon come from? Did I do that too?"

She must have developed a new level to her weirdness. Houdinism, teleportation, and now turning hot guys into dragons. This had to be a dream. Or drugs. Yes. Probably she was on drugs.

A very pretty woman who was just as curvy as Yvaine plopped down onto the couch beside her. "That's an interesting power you have. But no, that one's mine and he's just reacting to yours. One of these guys hulks out and the rest do too. Jakob doesn't like it much when anyone shifts inside the house unless there's danger."

"My what?" This lady's tone and attitude was all very blah for two dragons standing in her living room making mean eyes at each other.

"Your dragon." She said it like it was an everyday thing.

At least it wasn't Yvaine's fault. If there was at least three dragons and the woman sitting next to her thought that was normal, there must be more. Those dragons must go around kissing human women and then having to marry them. She guessed that was better than kidnapping them and eating them or forcing them to live in caves or castles waiting for knights in shining armor to rescue them.

"I have to admit, I don't really understand what's going on here." She obviously meant Jett when she said your dragon. He wasn't hers even a little bit. He was a wild thing that shouldn't ever be contained by the restriction of being owned. Or maybe dragon people culture was matriarchal as well as antiquated and because they were supposed to get married Yvaine now owned him. That thought made her wrinkle up her nose. Yuck.

Not at Jett. He was yummy. Which she totally should not be thinking right now.

The woman patted Yvaine's hand. "I feel ya. It took me a while to get a handle on the whole being a dragon's mate thing too."

"I understand the individual words your saying, but not when you put them together like that. Everything your saying has given me about a billion more questions than I had before being attacked by batstriches and seeing a dude turn into a dragon right before my eyes."

Miláčku, *take the girl and get out of here so I can kick the black rogue dragon's ass back into human form.*

Yvaine didn't like the sound of that, and neither did Jett if the growl rumbling around in his chest was any indication. But she didn't say anything - yet. She was ready to throw down if she had to. Throw down what, she didn't know. But something. Like this weird throw pillow.

The matriarch, or whoever, tsked the green dragon before the pillow fight with a dragon could ensue.

"Now, Jakey. I just redecorated this room and I'm already going to have to replace the Louis the someteenth chairs Jett squarshed. You two take your tussle outside. We're going to the kitchen to make some drinks." The woman turned back to Yvaine and asked, "Mimosas okay with you?"

"Uh. Sure. Let me just do one thing real quick." She stood up, sucked in a breath and wobbled waiting for the rainbow-colored spots in her vision to go away.

Yvaine? Jett lowered his head to her eye level and his hot breath felt good on her hair. She felt like she'd been cold for a really long time and was only now starting to warm back up. He took a step toward her and the sound of wood splintering sent the woman sitting next to her groaning.

Yvaine lifted her hand to keep Jett from trampling more of the expensive furniture in this luxury living room. "I'm okay. Just stood up too fast or something."

"Ooh." The woman grabbed Yvaine's arm and helped her sit back down. "You should take it easy. There was a giant hole in your chest a few minutes ago."

That sounded bad. And also, like she should be dead. "There was? I don't remember that."

Yvaine touched her shirt again and sure enough, there was a hole about the size of euro coin right through the unicorn's head.

That's why I brought you here. The green dragons' breath is healing.

Yvaine giggled and quickly covered her mouth. It was rude to thank someone for healing you by laughing. But seriously. Dragon's breath. She had that if she forgot to brush her teeth. The only thing that healed was the urge to kiss hot guys. The giggles burst out even though she was doing her best to hold them in.

"Uh-oh." The woman looked at her, gave a sympathetic smile which made Yvaine laugh even more. "Okay guys. Out you go. She's had all she can take for the morning. Shoo. I'll take it from here."

Jett and the green dragon grumbled but turned to leave. The green one shifted into a man while Jett just ducked his head and tried to fit through the same door. No way his big ole dragon butt was going anywhere, which was even more funny. Yvaine couldn't even contain her laughter with both hands now and she was out and out guffawing.

Jett turned to look at her with fire in his eyes. *This isn't funny.*

"But it is." She didn't want him stuck like this though so

reached her hand out and waved Jett toward her. He glared at her but lowered his head and stuck his snout into her palm. The black light shimmered over him and he was once again her hot fantasy man, all broody and frowny-faced.

He took her hand and kissed the inside of her palm. "Try to stay calm. No getting startled. You're safe here and I don't want to be caught unawares by another shift. Got it?"

Yvaine nodded and pressed her lips together so she didn't let any more giggles out. They came anyway. She simply couldn't stop them.

"Go with Ciara, now. Maybe she can help you get a handle on your magic."

"Okay." Giggle, giggle.

Ciara waved the men away. "Go outside and play."

Jakob shook his head, clearly amused by his wife or girl-friend or matriarch, what have you. "No castles today. But the rogue and I will be discussing the battle he had with the Black Dragon. If he's back we'll need all the intel we can get."

The men headed back outside and Ciara led Yvaine into a really lovely kitchen. It had warm colors in a French country vibe, an island with comfy padded stools, and smelled like fresh backed apple pie. If ever Yvaine had wondered like home felt like, this was it.

She sat on one of the stools while Ciara rooted around in the big built-in fridge. "We weren't exactly properly intro-duced. I'm Yvaine."

"I know. Aha. Here's that bottle I was saving for the next girls night." She lifted a bottle of champagne over her head and followed it up with a jug of orange juice.

"You do? Jett told you?" Just how long had she been unconscious?

She set the drinks on the counter along with a container of

juice, ripe strawberries, and opened a nearby cupboard with glassware. "No. The White Witch did, sort of. I get a vision of a lot of the mates when they get their necklaces. Mostly it's the Wyverns and their direct connections, like their second in commands. But Jett is neither of those, so I'm not sure why she showed me yours."

"Okay, back up. You get visions of what now?" Yvaine fingered the necklace she wore. Something about what Ciara said niggled a vague memory.

"Sorry." Ciara shook her head. "You'd think I of all people would remember what it's like to get thrown into this world, but sometimes I forget what the rest of the world knows about the dragon warriors and what they don't."

"Dragon warriors?" That term suited Jett perfectly. Yvaine popped a strawberry into her mouth and chewed imagining Jett in a uniform, brandishing a sword.

"Yeah. See, like that. Okay, here's the quick and dirty. Dragons exist. They fight evil, mostly in the form of demon dragons, although more recently also the Black Dragon who is the King of Hell and his sidekick, Ereshkigal, the Black Witch." She lifted her hand and ticked each thing she listed off. "There are four kinds of dragons, Green, Blue, Gold, and Red, plus Jett. He's a bit of an anomaly."

Kind of like Yvaine.

Ciara didn't stop. "The head of each dragon Wyr, which is like a clan, is called the Wyvern. You with me so far?"

Yvaine said "yes," but shook her head no.

"Let me keep going and then we'll go back and fill in the gaps and your questions. Here this will help." Ciara poured champagne and orange juice into a green champagne flute and handed it to Yvaine.

"A long time ago, I'm not sure how long ago we're talking,

but I think several centuries. There was the First Dragon. He hooked up with this lady called the White Witch and they had a bunch of half dragon half human babies."

Yvaine took a swig of the mimosa. Ciara was right. It did help.

"Their children became the first dragon Wyverns. They were all living happily for a while until some weird ass creatures that were half demon and half dragon started popping up around the world."

Finally, something she semi understood. "Oh. That must be the batstriches that attacked us."

"Batstriches?" Ciara half laughed and took a swig of her drink.

"Yeah. Big black creatures with wings like bats that are mean and go around of flapping their wings and pecking at everyone like horrible ostriches. Bat-ostriches." That sounded better in her head.

"That term fits them perfectly if you also include they like to eat babies, live in hell, are the minions of the Black Dragon and the Black Witch and can spit fire."

Crikies. "Yeah. Those guys. I didn't know about the eating babies part though."

"Yup. Evil incarnate." Ciara frowned and shook her head. "Anyway. The original dragon brothers decided they needed to protect mankind from the demon dragons and trained to become warriors. Now all dragons are born into the warrior culture and they've been fighting the demon dragons for a hella long time."

This called for a refill. Ciara was right there with her and topped off Yvaine's glass with champagne. "Okay. I think I'm with you. Although this is honestly blowing my mind. But what's the whole thing about mates. Jett said something about that he doesn't get mates. He tried to explain it means soul mate or something."

If Yvaine was honest with herself, she already knew what a mate was, didn't she? She couldn't understand how anyone thought she was soulmate material. A lonely girl, with no romantic experience, no home, no family, no friends didn't fit the bill. Yvaine was nothing like the glamourous woman who sipped champagne on a whim and embodied the very essence of beautiful confidence. Ciara was comfortable in her own skin, knew exactly who she was and so obviously loved life and herself.

Yvaine didn't hate herself or anything, she just couldn't understand what anyone else would see in her. Especially not a mythical warrior who happened to be hot underwear model material.

"Mate. Just one." Ciara held up her finger to indicate the singular, but Yvaine didn't miss the wooden ring on her fourth finger. It was anything but plain. It sparkled with a million green stones inlaid into its intricately carved vines, leaves, and flowers. This was no mere trinket. It held power. "And that's exactly what it is. Jakob is my soulmate. It's some sort of destiny, written in the stars, fate kind of thing."

Destiny. Fate. "Wait. You didn't get a choice?"

So many of life's choices had been either taken away from Yvaine or made for her. She didn't like the idea of who she fell in love with, or married, or mated to be out of her control too. What if she didn't want to be someone's mate? Dog gone it. She wanted that choice.

Ciara pursed her lips and nodded. The look was one of empathy, the words were not. "Yeah. No. I kind of fought against the idea at first too. But so far, fate hasn't been wrong."

Yvaine drained her glass and set it on the counter a little too hard. "You think I'm Jett's soul mate?"

"You are." Ciara looked Yvaine straight in the eye. Her eyes didn't waver, her body language set in the pure confidence in what she was saying.

Regardless of what Ciara thought, it wasn't going to happen. "I can't. I have to get to England, or Scotland. I'm not sure yet. I don't have time to be screwing around with some ancient war between mythical creatures."

The old feelings of being trapped were pressing in on her. This time it wasn't because of a small space, or even by monsters. She couldn't lose her cool. Jett would shift back into a dragon and be mad. Plus, if her disappearing act manifested, Ciara would see and look at her like a freak.

Little snowflakes appeared over Yvaine's head and drifted down. Each one that touched her skin and soaked in gave her a calming feeling. Well, maybe Ciara wouldn't think Yvaine was a weirdo, because she clearly had powers of her own. Still, Yvaine wasn't ready for any of this. She stood, knocking the stool over. "Sorry. Thank you for your hospitality, the wine was delicious. Please tell your dragon thank you for healing me. I'll be going now."

Ciara reached for her. "Yvaine, wait. I'm the one who should be sorry. I thought if I laid it all out for you it would be easier. Clearly I'm not as smart as I think I am."

Yvaine? Tell me what's wrong. You're safe. Everything is going to be okay.

No. It wasn't. None of this was okay. Why couldn't her life just be normal. Why couldn't she be normal? The magic inside of her pricked at her skin. For once she welcomed it, wanted to Houdini her way out of here. Where exactly did she think she would go? This lovely, warm, inviting kitchen wasn't a dark closet she'd been locked in at the convent. Ciara wasn't the Mother Superior that could never be pleased. Running away was not going to solve her problems.

She took a deep breath and consciously tried pushing the magic back down. She'd never done that before, but she also hadn't understood what it was or what it did either. Now that she knew there were other magical being in the universe, she didn't feel quiet as weird and freakish for having this ability inside of her.

"Wow." Ciara clapped her hands and smiled, wide-eyed. "Did you know you sparkle when you do whatever it is you were just doing? I've never seen magic like yours. It's beautiful."

Beautiful? Huh. "Umm, I didn't know. I've never seen it myself. I kind of thought it made me invisible."

Ciara came around the island and picked up the stool Yvaine had knocked over. She pushed it back, kind of like a peace offering. "That would be a cool trick. What else does it do? It doesn't appear to be elemental like mine. I didn't know there was any other kind of magic. Not that I'm and expert mind you."

Over and over Ciara had invited Yvaine into her world, never once making her feel like the odd man out. Yvaine was the one making herself feel like she didn't belong. Another thing she could push back inside. Okay. She could do this. No more running away. She sat back down and ate another strawberry like nothing out of the ordinary had just happened. "I don't really know. I've only recently tried using it consciously. Normally it just does its own thing and helps to keep me safe or escape when I'm in danger. What does elemental magic do?"

"You know, like the four elements. Earth, wind, water, fire."

Ciara waved her hand and the little houseplant next to the sink doubled in size and sprouted big pink flowers. Then it lifted up and floated across to the kitchen island on some sort of breeze. A tiny raincloud formed over the top of it and sprinkled onto the leaves and dirt, watering the plant. "I'm not as good with fire, unless like you I'm in danger."

"That's amazing. I don't think my magic works like that though. Do the dragons have magic too?" She remembered how Jett had used the darkness to hide them and had spit fire at the batstriches. Maybe he wasn't a fire breathing dragon and it was his kind of magic.

"Each of the dragon Wyrs have domain over one of the elements. You can probably guess that reds have fire, blues have water, golds are wind and sky, and our Green dragons are earth. I think if Jakob didn't have his warriors to lead, he'd be content rolling around in the mud all day."

She hadn't mentioned black dragons.

"I heard that, *miláček*." Jakob walked into the kitchen and wrapped his arms around Ciara, snuggling her from behind. "You enjoy a good mud bath as much as I do."

She laughed. "It does make my skin all rosy."

"As do the many orgasms I give you when we are cleaning up." Jakob nipped at Ciara's ear, then must have remembered Yvaine was standing right across from them. He raised his head from nuzzling the ornate green dragon tattoo at Ciara's neck. "Jett wishes you to join him in the garden."

He probably wanted her to turn him back into a human again. She'd pushed back her power a moment ago. Maybe she could also learn to control whatever it was that kept forcing Jett to shift into his dragon form when she got scared. She wished there was someone who could teach her. "Okay. I'll just go find him then."

Jakob nodded. "There is a woman in the nearby village who works for the dragons from time to time who goes by the name Mrs. Bohacek. I suggested to Jett that you two go see her. Perhaps she can help you learn to use your magic. But I have warned Jett that if the demon dragons who are seeking him show up he must leave immediately. I will not have their evil threaten the people under my protection."

MATE HER, DUMMY

*M*ark her.
Claim her.
Mate her.

The words kept going round and round and round in his head driving him more insane by the minute. Jakob wanted to grill him on everything he knew about the Black Dragon's movements, the recent attack, and why Ereshkigal would be acting on her own. That last part had been news to him.

It was a huge revelation that the Cage, the Gold Wyvern and his mate, the mermaid from hell, had born twin babies. Throw in the fact that the Black Witch had shown up to steal said babies and Jett should care a whole lot. The first children of dragons in hundreds of years. A boy and a girl. Until now there were no daughters of dragons. It meant someone had broken one of Ereshkigal's curses.

Hell must be in chaos. His father's stronghold on the African continent had been destroyed. Ereshkigal's powers were weakening. Discord between the rulers of hell. All signs said this was the perfect time for him to strike.

It wasn't that he didn't care. He did. His brothers had suffered long enough. Jett had tried everything, given up everything to find a way to free them and kill the Black Dragon. Instead of continuing his search for the last key to making everything he'd scrabbled his way out of hell to make happen, he was day dreaming about a woman.

He couldn't concentrate even a little bit on anything but her scent, her eyes, her touch of magic. A day ago all he could think about was finding the cure for the curse so he could save his brethren from the pits of hell and their servitude to his father. He'd spent months avoiding the dragon warriors and hunting for the spell that would change everything.

Mark her.

Claim her.

Mate her.

Jett paced back and forth in the elaborate garden behind the Wyvern's villa. Yvaine had freaked the fuck out while talking to Ciara and he'd shifted back into his dragon form. Jakob had laughed at him. Once Jett confirmed that Yvaine wasn't in any danger he'd picked a fight with the green dragon. Jakob had been all too happy to oblige. They'd flown through the air clawing and lashing at each other, but not doing any real harm. Jett kept his fire to himself. He still needed the Wyverns as allies.

The exercise had blown off a little steam, but he knew something that would blow off a whole lot more.

Yvaine, under him, crying his name as he fucked her into coming over and over. The dragon part of him reveled in the thought. It wanted to do exactly that. To claim her as its own. As its mate. That pure instinctual part of him didn't understand that he could fuck all the women in the world, he could mark them all with his bite, he could declare for all of Dragonkind that she belonged to him, and none of it would make her his true mate.

Not without a soul to give to her. He'd even try to steal one if it would make a difference. He already knew from experience that it didn't.

"Jett?"

The tinkling sound of her voice pushed his mood even darker. Why did she have to be so damn beautiful? Even with dirt on her face, a stray piece of hay in her messy hair, and a fucking hole in her ridiculous unicorn shirt she took his breath away. He couldn't breathe fire to roast a marshmallow if he wanted to.

What? He snapped at her. If he pretended to hate her he could distance himself from all these damn feelings.

She took a step back with confusion in her eyes. Good. Yeah, he was going to be that asshole. If she didn't like being around him she would be more motivated to figure out how to quit controlling his shift all the sooner. Then he could leave her behind and get back to plotting the demise of the Black Dragon.

"Jakob said we should go into town and see a woman who can help me figure out my powers."

Then let's go already.

Yvaine frowned and narrowed her eyes at him but didn't say anything. She walked away following the gravel path that led out of the estate. It was only a couple of miles to the town. Jett had seen that from the sky. Walking would take them much longer than he had the patience for.

Mark her. Claim her.

Grr.

Hurry the fuck up.

She stopped dead in her tracks and put her hands on her

hips. "What's got your snoot in a root? I'm walking as fast as I can. If you hadn't noticed I missed breakfast, didn't get my coffee, and oh, yeah I was murdered earlier today. I'd like a little slack if you don't mind."

She was even more beautiful all riled up like this. Her breathing had ratcheted up, the breeze blew tendril of her hair around, and the rosiness she'd had in her cheeks the first time he'd seen her was back with a vengeance. He wanted nothing more than to take her in his arms and kiss the daylights out of her. He was so fucked.

Jett lowered his head right down to her eye level and bared his teeth at her like he was going to take a bite. He wanted to, badly.

"Back off, buster." Yvaine poked him right on the nose and he was back to man form in less than a blink. She continued to stare up at him, the fire in her eyes reflecting his own. Hers was from anger.

His was pure unadulterated lust.

"Stop doing that," she whispered. "You're confusing me."

"Stop doing what?" He took a step closer so she had to tilt her head back to look up at him.

"Looking at me like that. One second your all crabby and the next I think you want to..." When her voice trailed off her little pink tongue darted between her lips, sliding across the bottom one leaving it shiny and wet.

He wanted to know what else was wet. "What do you think I want to do to you, Yvaine? This?"

Jett cupped her head and lowered his mouth to hers. He slid his lips over hers, teasing them both waiting to see if she would let him take the kiss even farther. Her little gasp was all the signal he needed. He took advantage of her parted lips and slipped the tip of his tongue between them, tasting her again for the first time. The flavor of strawberries and sunshine flooded his senses. He needed so much more.

He got it when she wrapped her arms around his neck and sucked his bottom lip into her mouth. Jett lost all sense of time and space. There was only her and him and this fiery magic between them. She moved into his body and he wrapped his arms around her back, pulling her even closer. Their mouths moved together, their tongues danced with each other, and their breaths synced until he didn't know where he stopped and she began.

Swirls of black light wrapped around them and sparks of fire exploded behind his eyes amping up his need for her. Jett's wings exploded from his back and he wrapped them behind her, creating a tight cocoon around them to keep her safe from the dangers lurking in the world.

Mark her. Claim her.

Yes. He wanted the rest of the world to know if they messed with Yvaine, they would feel his wrath. Because she was his. Curse or no. Soul or no, Yvaine was his. Jett broke the kiss wanting to work his way down to her throat, but she pulled him back to her and took what she wanted from him. One more deep, lingering kiss that she got to say when it ended.

"It was either that or eat me." She smiled against his mouth and pecked him on the lips again.

"But I do want to eat you." That too made her gasp and he loved seeing her eyes sparkle with the anticipation. That made it all the harder to say, "I don't know how to do this, Yvaine. I know how to fight, I know how to fuck, but I don't know how to--"

"Shh." She shook her head. "I don't either. Do we have to? Everything else is so complicated at the moment. Let's just make this part easy. I like kissing you. I'd like to do it more. Everything else about today has scared the ever living shinola out of me. Except you. I don't know why. I kind of don't care at this point."

"I don't scare you?" The darkness of his soul sure as shit made him worried sometimes.

She rubbed her thumb over his cheek and across his lips. "You've surprised me a few times, but you're one of the good guys. I don't have any reason to fear you."

One of the good guys. He wasn't. If he'd had a heart, it would have broken right then. She might be his. But he could never have her. Jett opened his wings and the rays of sunshine hit him right in the eye so that he had to turn his face and look away. His wings shifted, tucking themselves back into his body where they belonged. He took one last second to stare down at Yvaine, imprinting this shining memory so that when the bleak lonely days that were ahead darkened his days he could take it back out and savor what could have been.

Jett smiled down at her hoping the muscles of his face didn't betray the gut-wrenching sadness he kept inside. "Let's go find this woman so you can learn to use your powers, huh?"

"Okay." She took his hand in hers and he didn't have the strength to let go. Not yet.

They found the shop that Jakob had described and a little bell rang when they opened the door. Jett sniffed the air, searching for the scent of whatever kind of being this Mrs. Bohacek might be. For a moment he thought he smelled something familiar. Jett pushed Yvaine behind him, and scanned the room for her enemies.

The beast that had been at the pub last night, the one that had been lying in wait for Yvaine was here. In the same breath the scent was gone and his nostrils filled with old smoke, fresh cut grass, ocean water, and warm desert breeze. If all of those smells were here, this woman had helped many a dragon. Perhaps she was also counsel to other paranormal creatures. Even the ones that hunted his Yvaine. Just what was she?

A tall man, with battle scars on his face and a prosthetic arm stepped up behind the little counter and greeted them. "Hello there, Yvaine. Nice to see you again. Welcome."

Yvaine stuck her head out from behind Jett's back and looked at the man. "Do I know you? Have we met before?"

The guy didn't take his eyes off Yvaine. He didn't even acknowledge Jett. "We have young lady. Come in, come in. Can I offer you a refreshment? My lovely mate left us some fresh baked lemon scones. They're vegan."

"Ooh. Yeah, I'm starving. Thanks." Despite Jett's arm holding her back, Yvaine jumped at the plate of baked goods. She bit into one before Jett could warn her not to. "Mmm. Fro moof. Franksh."

Clearly the only danger here was of Yvaine spitting scone pieces at her host by talking with her mouth full.

"You're welcome. Please have a seat." The man indicated to a tall chair and a little breeze pushed it back for her to sit in. "I have good news and bad news."

"Give us the bad news." Jett folded his arms and waited for this guy to tell him Mrs. Bohacek couldn't help them.

"First the good news," he said once again completely ignoring Jett. "I know how you can break your curse."

"Her curse? Yvaine is cursed?" Great. That must be what had her screwing with his shifting abilities. If this man knew how to break Yvaine's curse, he might have knowledge that would break the demon dragon's curse too.

"Uhh, I don't know what you're talking about. What curse?" This time she waited until she finished asking her question before taking another bite of her scone.

Jett reached for one of them and she slapped his hand away. He needed to remember to feed her more often.

"The one keeping you from knowing who and what you are. The same one that has every magic dealer this side of the Mississippi hunting you since you escaped the evil clutches of the convent."

Yvaine paused with her next bite of scone halfway to her mouth. "Holy shirt. I knew it. There were people after me. I was trying not to be paranoid, but it's true. Did you imply evil nuns? Did they curse me? They didn't seem wicked. Maybe Mother Superior, but the rest of them were god-fearing women who cared for orphans like me."

The man laughed. "You're right. They aren't malevolent. Nuns just always creeped me out. Can't charm their pants off even if you tried. That ain't right. But don't tell Mrs. Bohacek I said that. She'd be mad and I wouldn't be getting any nookie tonight."

Yvaine grinned and winked at him conspiratorially. Jett didn't like that even a little bit. She didn't need to have secrets with anyone but him. He moved closer to her and put a hand on her shoulder, playing with her hair so this guy would know exactly who she belonged to.

"I won't. Promise. Where is Mrs. Bohacek? Ciara and Jakob thought she might be able to help me with my magic. I keep turning poor Jett into a dragon and back again. I don't get how any of this works."

The man glanced down at the now empty plate avoiding looking at Yvaine. "That's the bad news, I'm afraid. She, uh, couldn't be here."

Yeah. He knew it. There was something fishy going on here.

"Oh. Shoot. Why not?" Yvaine's disappointment filled his nostrils. Dammit. He was going to have to teach her not to rely on anyone but herself.

"Well." He sighed long and loud. "That's my fault. She's mad at me and left in a huff when she heard you were coming. In fact, she didn't really want me to be here when you got here either. I had to make certain promises."

"What did you do to make her mad?" She gasped. "Wait. Did I do something?"

"No, sweetness. She likes you. It's the only reason we're talking instead of me getting my ass chewed. Again. She's mad about something that happened a long time ago." For the first time since they walked into the shop the man lifted his eyes to Jett.

What the fuck? He didn't do anything to these people. He didn't even know who they were. "Come on, Yvaine. Let's go. This guy can't help you."

Once again, he was ignored. The man slipped something out of the pocket on his shirt. "There is a sure-fire way to break any curse, Yvaine."

Hold up. They could stay one more minute. This was the information he'd been waiting on last night.

"You have to find the unicorns. Curses are dark magic and unicorns come from pure white magic."

Yvaine snickered. "I freaking love unicorns. You're telling me they are real?"

Even Jett didn't know that for sure. Only the fairytale that their blood was magical. He'd never seen one, heard of one just hanging around. If anyone had known of their existence and what it could mean to Jett, it would have been Geshtianna. Not like she had been forthright with her information. If there was even a chance this mythical creature could save him and his brothers, they had to find it.

The man nodded, very serious and Yvaine looked as dumbstruck as Jett felt. "I mean, I guess if dragons are, they could be too."

"Yes. Their blood can break any curse almost instantly."

Jett's own blood rushed through his ears, whoosh, whoosh, whoosh-whoosh. Break any curse. Instantly.

"Eww, no. Are you sure we need its blood? I wouldn't want to hurt it."

Jett would. He'd bleed the thing dry if it meant saving Yvaine from whatever was hunting her. He couldn't be there for her forever. She needed to be free. If sacrificing one creature meant he could also save his brothers from their cursed life in hell. He would absolutely do it. "Where can we find a unicorn?"

"That's a decision you'll have to make and sooner than I think you'll want to." He slid a tattered brown piece of paper across the table to Yvaine. "This is where you'll find what you're looking for."

"Really? A map to a unicorn?" Yeah, and he had a bridge he could sell her too.

"I have given you everything you need." The man changed his voice into a weird stage whisper. "But sometimes you have to mark and claim the gifts in your life for yourself. So everyone knows they are yours."

Yvaine raised an eyebrow at the guy. "You mean like X marks the spot?"

He stepped back from the counter and continued speaking in that whisper, but as if he were addressing the whole room. Even though Jett and Yvaine were the only ones here. "When there is something you know belongs to you and you to it, even when you don't think you deserve it, you must do everything in your power to hold that precious gift close, protect it with all your heart and soul. You know what to do. Do it already."

"Uh. Okay. I guess. Thanks for the scones, the map, and that bit of cryptic advice. We'll just be going now." Yvaine held the paper to her chest and backed away toward the door.

Jett waited for her to slip outside before confronting the man. "Who are you?"

The guy still didn't look at Jett. What a complete tool. A to punch arm or the face would get his attention. Jett clenched his fist, readying to sock the guy when he up and disintegrated into a thousand colorful petals that swirled around the room. Half of them smacked Jett in the face. He grabbed a few out of his eyes. These were no soft bits of flowers, they were hard as diamonds. In the palm of his hand Jett rolled six of the things over and over. There was a rainbow of colors, red, green, blue, gold, white, and black.

Scales. These were dragon scales.

He glanced around the room looking for any other clue to confirm his suspicions about the identity of the man. The door reopened and Yvaine stuck her head in. "You coming, Jett?"

"Do you know who that was we, I mean you, were just talking to?" Jett stared at his hand and lifted it for her to see.

"I assumed it was Mr. Bohacek. Where did he go?" She stepped back into the little shop and glanced down into Jett's hand.

The scales there turned to nothing more than a handful of rainbow glitter. It lifted into the air on a breeze and landed on Yvaine, most of it right on the soft skin of her neck. It sparkled in a ray of light coming in through the only window in the place. Jett swore they landed in a pattern of an arrow that flashed at him.

Mark her. Claim her. Mate her.

Jett could resist no more. He may be condemning them both, but Yvaine held in her hand the cure for any curse, so maybe they could both be saved. He pulled her into his arms and kissed her like they were the stars in a blockbuster Hollywood movie. She squeaked in surprise, then melted into him, taking his face in her hands and returning every bit of fervor.

Jett took a long deep breath. "You are mine, Yvaine. Mine."

He pushed the chain of the necklace she wore aside and it too turned to dragon scales in his hands. They joined the swirls of black light and fiery red sparks in the air around them. If they spelled out the words 'mark her' in the air their intent would be any clearer than it already was. Someone or something was conspiring for the two of them to be together.

"Jett? I need you. Please. Kiss me again. Make me yours." Yvaine's soft plea made his mouth water for her.

Jett pressed his lips to her throat, gave it a gentle kiss and then let his dragon's fangs extend. He scraped them across her skin being careful not to break her tender flesh, but he had to leave his mark on her. He gently bit down and sucked hard, pulling and lapping at the wound he was making on her.

"Jett, holy, oh, wow, Jett." She trembled in his arms and her knees gave out. She clung to him and he held her tight until he was satisfied her throat would bear the mark of his love for her.

Love?

No. It wasn't love he felt. It couldn't be. He didn't know how to love.

NO SOUL, NO SOULMATE

*H*oly. Cow. Bells. Or maybe that was church bells ringing in her ears. There were definitely angels singing.

Whatever Jett had just done to her had turned her into a big ole pile of flaming girl goo. She couldn't talk, she couldn't think, she couldn't think about talking. All she could do was hold him in her arms and hope that he would never ever stop.

"Yvaine? I'm sorry if I hurt you." His voice was dark and husky, but with an edge of worry.

He didn't have anything to be worried about. "Don't stop. Whatever you're doing feels incredible. Do it some more."

She pushed her hands into his beautiful black hair and pulled him back for much, much more kissing or maybe this was what they called necking.

He stopped before he his lips and teeth touched her again and hissed out a breath. "That's not what I thought would happen."

"That I want you to make out with me some more? Why? I thought we did a pretty good job of it." Granted she didn't have a ton of experience. He was her first real kiss and all. They both seemed to like it though. That was good. If she was honest with herself, she hoped kissing would lead to other fun activities she knew she'd been missing out on.

"Not that. I do want to spend a lot more time doing that." He licked his lips and stared at her mouth making her go all weak in the knees again. "And a whole lot more than just kissing you. That's not what I'm talking about. Look."

Ooh. Yay. He did want to do naughty things with her. She could hardly wait. But where were they going now? Jett took her over to the window and pointed to her reflection. On her neck, where Jett had gotten deliciously aggressive with his kissing, she thought she'd see a big ole hickey. Instead there was a sparkling black dragon with eyes that literally looked like they were little balls of fire.

She reached up and touched it. Her skin was smooth, the mark as much a part of her as anything else on her body. "Jett, it's beautiful. Thank you."

Jett blinked, surprised by her appreciation. "Yvaine. No. I'm afraid I've cursed you as I am. That mark binds us together. I've claimed you and no other dragon or any other beast in the supernatural world will ever want to mate you."

"That's so sweet." She'd never felt a connection to anyone else like this. Several times she'd tried to walk away from him, told herself she was feeling nothing more than a crush. Ciara implied that it was more. Yvaine wanted very badly to believe that. She'd never belonged to anyone and no one had ever belonged to her. She'd pushed down that particular unmet need her entire life, pretending that it didn't matter that she didn't have any family, no one to love.

But it did matter.

Jett scowled at their reflections. "You don't get it. I have nothing to give you. I'm a rogue with no Wyr. A bastard of the King of Hell. I'm cursed. I have no soul to be your mate."

Yvaine turned from the reflection to make sure that Jett didn't misunderstand anything she said to him. "You listen to me. I don't care about your past. I barely have one myself. I've never known my family or who I am. Today I found out I don't even know what I am. None of that matters. Because I like who I am when I'm with you."

She didn't know that was true until the words came out of her mouth. Until recently she'd been a scared little girl who used her special power to hide and run away from people. With Jett, she could be something different, someone better than before. Instead of being the girl who ran, she could be the girl who fought back.

Jett closed his eyes in a very long blink. "What are you talking about? Since we met you've been hunted by mermen, another beast I haven't yet identified, the Black Dragon, and you were killed by a demon dragon. Killed. Your life has become a complete shit show in the past twenty-four hours."

Her life had been that way long before yesterday. She just hadn't realized it. Now it was filled with magic, and the potential of love and family. She was going to embrace it all. "Really? Mermen. Cool."

The ever-present fires in Jett's eyes changed from being fueled by fear and anger, to the tiniest bit of amusement. "That's what you got out of what I just said to you?"

"No." How could she put this? She wanted him to understand that he wasn't to blame and that they were in this together now. "I also got that you've been helping and protecting me even though I stole your beer and basically sexually harassed you in the first minute we met. So I was murdered a little bit. It turned out fine."

There was his smile. He had no idea how it lit up his whole face. How it took her breath away. "I don't think one can be murdered a little bit."

She pointed to the hole in her shirt. "Case in point."

He glared at that hole for far too long, the angry fires returning to his eyes. "I still have nothing to give you. I don't have a soul, Yvaine. How can I be your soul mate without a fucking soul?"

She didn't believe that for a hot second. Someone had taught him that he was worthless. How could he not see how shiny and bright the fire inside of him was? She wasn't going to convince him here and now of it. She'd work on him for as long as it took. "Soul, schmoal. I'll just share mine with you."

For the briefest of moments, the fire in Jett's eyes burned blue and then white hot. If she hadn't been staring into them so deeply, she would have missed it. They flickered back to his usual reddish yellow flame and he blinked at her, twice, three times. "I don't think that how it works, love."

"Aww. You called me love." She was going to have to come up with a pet name for him too. How exciting.

"Yvaine." He growled her name and it sent lots of fun shivers through her.

"Jett." She did her best to match his tone, but couldn't do it. She was too giddy with these new-found feelings for him to sound lustfully cranky.

His eyes flicked back and forth between hers, searching for something. Maybe that soul business. "I'm still afraid I've cursed you to the darkness with me."

She tried to refute him again, but he held up his hand to stop her and all she got out was a tiny grunt. He dropped his fingers to her mouth and caressed her lips. "But I don't think I can give you up. I guess we'd better go find that unicorn and break all the curses we can with it."

Finally. Uh-oh. He'd said curses. Plural. Maybe unicorns had blood banks. "Are there more curses than the one that's on me, that you want to break?"

"Yes." He nodded and looked like he was choosing his words carefully. "When you came into the bar last night, I was waiting for a magic dealer. He was supposed to give me information on how to break the curse on my brothers."

Whoa. Built in family. "You have brothers? Are they all as handsome as you?"

"You've met them. Well, some of them."

The only other dragons they'd met was the green one and the big black one that had tried to capture and or kill them. Crud. He was definitely related to that black one. Duh. He had said something about it being the King of Hell and also that he was the bastard son. Now she was putting two and two and two together. "I have, when? Is it Jakob?"

Please be Jakob, please be Jakob.

"No." He swallowed and looked at her like he didn't want to say. "The demon dragons are my brethren."

"Uh. The batstriches? Brothers from another mother, I take it?"

"We are all children of the Black Dragon, the King of Hell. Some are born beyond any hope of real life, but others, like the one who tried to kill you, I think I can save them. They still retain their sense of self, they can communicate, and they are waiting for me to begin the revolution to rescue them from life as a minion, forced to battle the dragon warriors in the name of Kur-Jara and his vengeance on Dragonkind."

Yvaine raised her arms in the air. "*Viva la Resistance.*"

Jett shook his head but she saw the smile on his face too. "Let's see that map and find out where we're going tomorrow."

She handed him the brown piece of paper. "Tomorrow?"

He took it, but didn't bother unfolding it. "Yes. My brethren have waited centuries to be freed. They can wait one more night. Tonight, I'm taking you back to the Green Wyvern's villa, begging his bride for a room for the evening, where I can be sure we won't have any distractions from friends nor foe."

"Umm, because you're tired and want to rest for our journey?" He didn't look tired. She wasn't. She was invigorated and could've danced all night. And still have asked for more.

"Not even a little. Because I want you in my bed, under me, moaning my name as I make you come over and over until we are both exhausted and satisfied."

"Oh." She said that instead of a squee, which was what she was really feeling inside. Was now a good time to tell him she hadn't ever done any of the coming and moaning someone's name thing before? Probably not. He'd figure it out soon enough. Stay cool. "That sounds like...fun."

"I'm going to make it much more than fun for you, love."

There he went again calling her love. Did he love her? He couldn't. Not yet. Maybe having sex would help her figure that out. They did call it making love. She got a thrill every time he called it fucking. She really wanted to experience fucking. They could do making love later. "Do we have to wait until tonight?"

"If I could I would fly you back to the villa and be inside of you in the next six minutes. But the nature of our curses means we will be walking back. I won't have you vulnerable where there are no wards. This town is under the Green Wyr protection, but it isn't as safe as their home. When I'm fucking you I don't want to worry about demon dragons popping up. They will never come close to you ever again. Not until we have broken their curse."

"I'll race ya." Yvaine bolted through the door and took off running. She wouldn't have the stamina to last very long before she either got a stitch in her side or wore out. Even better if he caught her.

Yvaine. Don't you know better than to run from a predator, naughty girl?

Oops she must have changed him in her excitement. The shop they'd met Mr. Bohacek in was right at the edge of town and as soon as she hit the open road, she sped up to sprint as fast as she could. Living in the convent, she hadn't been allowed to run like this. It was almost as exhilarating as Jett's kisses.

Her hair whipped out behind her and her muscles woke up, the blood rushing through them, for the first time in her life. "Bet you can't catch me, dragon."

Run, my mate. Because when I do capture you, you won't be going anywhere for a long time.

Yvaine laughed with the pure joy of being in the wide open country-side, free as a bird. She felt like she could fly. Jett flew over her head and his shadow passed beside her. He swooped down like he was going to grab her up in his talons, but she darted to the side giggling like a fool. Before she knew it, the villa and its gardens came into view. She didn't want this chase to end, but she did want what was going to happen when Jett caught her to start as soon as possible. She slowed down and came to a stop in front of the main entryway to the house, bending at the waist and breathing hard.

Jett landed beside her and bowed his head. *Whatever you*

are, running is in your blood. I truly couldn't catch you and believe me I tried.

Yvaine half laughed, half sucked in deep long breaths. She threw her arms around Jett's dragony neck and when he had lips again she kissed them. "I've never done that before. It was fun. My heart is beating so fast but I hardly feel tired."

He lifted her up into his arms and kicked the big wooden door open, carrying her across the threshold.

"Oh gosh, you can't carry me like this, I'm too heavy." Princesses got carried around, not chubby orphan girls. Secretly she loved that he hadn't even grunted with effort when he grabbed her up.

"Not even a little bit." He strolled into the main room and toward a big staircase that led up to a second level.

Ciara popped her head around the corner probably wondering if Jett was in here breaking his furniture again. Jakob wasn't far behind. Neither got to say a word before Jett bounded up the stairs.

"We require a room for the evening. We'll be leaving in the morning."

"Last room on the left." Ciara hollered up behind them. "I'll do a little sound-proofing ward on it to give you some privacy. I'll have cook send up snacks later. Have fun storming the castle."

It didn't take Jett long to find the room and he didn't even have to kick that door open. Yvaine gasped when she saw the opulent room. It was decorated in deep reds, with a soft love seat in front of a huge fireplace, and a bed that was bigger than most rooms she'd ever stayed in. He set her down at the foot of the mattress and pushed her back into the plush bedding.

"The door," she whispered.

Jett growled but crossed back and slammed the door shut. When he turned back around his lids were half-lowered in the most sensual look on a man she'd ever seen. He was so damn sexy and she wanted him, on top of her, inside of her.

He was already stalking toward her but she decided it would be fun to lift a finger and motion him over with a come-hither look. She was probably doing this all wrong. Virgins were supposed to be quiet, shy, and reticent. Yvaine didn't want to be any of those things. She didn't even know who said she had to be. So she wasn't going to.

She knew she didn't have a perfect body. He seemed to like her anyway. Maybe she'd look dumb trying to be sexy, but he made her feel like she already was. "Take off your shirt, dragon."

He crossed his arms and yanked the t-shirt over his head, tossing it to the floor behind him. Yvaine was going to spend hours running her hands and maybe her tongue over every single muscle in his chest and abs. Dear sweet heaven. She was also going to spend a very long time kissing every single one of the scars marring each of his shoulders. Whatever had made those marks had happened long ago and must have been very painful.

"Your turn, Yvaine. Take off your shirt, and then your jeans, and everything else you have on so I can lick, and kiss, and suckle every part of your body. I will claim you from head to toe and all the fun places in between."

Yes, yes, and more yes. But she wanted to make every part of this experience last as long as possible. She'd been waiting for it for years. "I think it would be more fun if you took them off of me."

"If I do that you won't have anything to wear tomorrow

because I'm going to shred them if you're still wearing anything by the time I touch you. I want nothing between us."

She didn't even have time to get her hands under the hem of her shirt. He was in front of her, grabbing the collar and made good on his promise. The tattered pieces fell down her arms and to the bedspread.

"I warned you," he said and reached for her bra.

"That shirt was trash anyway." But bras in her size were harder to come by. She could probably borrow clothes from Ciara in the morning, but it would be weird to ask for undergarments too. She slipped straps off and reached behind to unclasp it. She tossed it to the side and reveled in Jett's sudden intake of breath.

If there was one thing she did like about having extra curves, it was her boobs. She had a great rack.

Jett leaned down and cupped each of her breasts in his big strong hands. His skin was hot to the touch and she couldn't wait for him to put her hands on her everywhere. She was already feeling warm, especially between her legs. He was going to send her up in flames.

He rubbed a thumb over each of her nipples and lowered his head to her chest. His lips touched down directly over her heart, right where the circular scar sat on her chest. He kissed it, softly, and whispered into her skin. "I'm sorry I didn't protect you from this."

Yvaine ran her hands over his shoulders, feeling each of the long scars there all the way down to her soul. "I'm sorry I wasn't there to protect you from this."

His eyes shimmered, dark around the edges and fiery hot inside. "Love. You couldn't have been. They happened a long time ago. Someday soon I will exact my revenge for both of our scars."

He was being far too serious for the amount of fun she wanted them to have tonight. "Mmm. Whisper more sweet nothings like that into my ear."

"I'll never understand how I got so lucky to have fate bring me to you."

That whole destiny thing still bothered her. She was here with Jett by her own choice. "Fate can suck it. I'm the one who found you, remember?"

"I'll never forget." Jett climbed up on the bed and over her, pushing her arms over her head. He licked and nipped at the skin beneath her shiny new dragon mark and lowered himself onto her, pressing her into the bed. Yowzah. He aligned her hips with his and ground against her.

Yvaine wrapped her legs around the backs of his thighs holding him right where she needed him most. Screw taking their time. She wanted to touch and feel and see what he was hiding in his jeans that was making her wet. "Pants, take off your pants, and mine while you're at it."

"Teasing you is more fun than I expected it would be. I think I'll work my way slowly down your body, spending lots of time sucking on each of these lush nipples before I take off any more of your clothes."

"Meanie."

"You have no idea." He chuckled and blew a scorching breath across one breast before drawing it into his mouth. He lashed it with his tongue and Yvaine literally saw stars behind her eyelids.

She squirmed beneath him trying to free her arms so she could take her own stupid jeans off. If his mouth on her breast blew her mind, what else could he do with that talented tongue of his. Try as she might, he didn't let her move an inch. "I need to feel you. All of you."

He hummed his agreement, but still didn't let her up. No, instead he tortured her with his mouth, making her moan when he switched from one nipple to the other. "That feels so good. Can I try it on you?"

That got his attention. He lifted his head and licked his lips. "Maybe later."

"How about now? Now would be good. Isn't it mine turn to melt your brain?" She couldn't wait to explore every inch of his body.

"We're nowhere near that point yet. But I'll concede a little." Jett released her arms, but only so he could kiss his way down her stomach, swirl his tongue around her belly button and rip open the fly of her jean.

There went one more piece of clothing she wouldn't be putting back on in the morning. Only one more left. He yanked the jeans down her legs and tossed them to the floor with all the other tattered pieces of fabric.

"Yvaine. Are there seriously little unicorns all over your panties?"

Duh. "Yes. What else would there be? Dragons?"

"This dragon would rather be inside of them." He pushed her legs open and kissed a very strategically placed unicorn that sent all kinds of lava pouring through her body. He used his teeth, gripping the material between them and yanked the scraps off of her.

"Ouch." Having her panties ripped off sounded more fun than it was. She was going to have welts.

"Let me kiss it and make it better." Jett nibbled his way from the inside of her thigh, until she was going mad waiting for him to actually kiss her. She pushed her hands into his hair and gripped it tight not letting him move a centimeter. Finally his tongue pressed along her folds and he growled long and low. "You fucking taste like sweet cherries, brown sugar, and the ripest peaches. I will never get enough of you."

Jett lapped at her, swirling his tongue around and around, up and down, until her legs were trembling and she couldn't think straight. "Please, Jett. Please don't stop. I'm so close."

He flicked the tip of his tongue over her clit and then sucked it between his lips, scraping his teeth over the ultra sensitive bud. Her hips bucked trying to get more of his rough touch and she cried out his name. "Jett, oh yes. Jett, Jett."

Those stars she saw earlier exploded into supernovas that collapsed in on themselves sucking every bit of air from the room. Her whole universe shrunk to only Jett between her legs and then exploded sending her consciousness into a thousand million pieces when her orgasm slammed into her body sending her so far over the edge, she wasn't sure she would ever come back.

DUCK ME, BABE

Yvaine wanted her turn to melt Jett's mind, but it was already mush and he hadn't even come yet. Fuck, she hadn't even touched him. He was on the verge of absolute bliss from hearing her little moans and gasps of pleasure. The way she gripped his hair, pulling on his scalp, guiding him to exactly the way she wanted his mouth on her had his cock rock hard and weeping to be inside of her.

Geshtianna and her succubus coven had taught him well how to give a woman pleasure, but it had always been just part of the act. Give pleasure so he could take his own. He'd never gotten anything more out of it than being allowed to get his own rocks off. It had never been like this.

Yvaine squirmed and cried out his name, pressing her delicious wet cunt into his mouth. He fucking loved it. She tasted like no other woman he'd ever been with. Literally she was the flavor of sweet berries and brown sugar and cotton god-damned candy. But when she climaxed, it was like drug-induced rainbows exploded in his head. Her orgasm was the best time he'd ever had in or out of bed.

Her body went limp under his mouth and Jett gave her one more long lick and dropped his forehead to the mattress, breathing just as hard as she did, trying to regain his composure.

The tiniest giggle erupted from her. "I think I've been doing orgasms wrong, because that was...something else."

Jett nipped at her inner thigh and then crawled up onto the bed and over her. He took her mouth in a long hard kiss and she moaned when he pushed his tongue into her, letting her taste herself. Not stopping for even a moment to let her catch her breath he reached between her legs and teased her entrance with two fingers. "We've only just begun. I intend to watch you come apart for me this time. Your orgasms are intoxicating."

"Again? Already? That one was so overwhelming, I don't see how I could possibly--"

Jett pushed his fingers through her slick folds and homed in on her hard nub. When he pinched and stroked the soft flesh her mouth popped open into a wide O and her eyes crossed. Mmm. Yes. That's what he wanted to see. He kissed her again, tracing her lips with his tongue and then propped himself up on one elbow to watch her come for him. He paid very close attention to the way her body responded to his touch and repeated every stroke that had her moaning.

"Oh man. Oh, oh. Jett, what are you doing to me? I...I." He swirled his thumb over her clit and her hips lifted off the bed.

Her eyes shut and she thrashed her head from side to side. She gripped the comforter tight in each fist and arched her back. Her tongue snaked out and she bit down on her lip stifling her cries.

"Come for me again, love. Let me hear your cry out my name."

She thrashed and tried to close her legs and he didn't let her get away for even a second. "Come for me right now, Yvaine. Give me your orgasm. It's mine, only mine."

She threw her head back and her entire body shook, contracting with the force of her climax. She didn't scream his name this time, her voice was a hoarse cry. Jett replied in kind, her name on his lips as a wave of pleasure hit him. Holy fuck, she was projecting her orgasm onto him, pouring the rush of feel good chemicals and hormones into his body. They were already so tightly connected that he couldn't imagine what it would be like when he finally brought their bodies together and made them one.

They both gasped for air, panting hard. Jett sucked in a long deep breath working to get himself back under control.

"Where did you learn to do that?"

Oh shit. He definitely should not tell her about fucking around with any succubus. "You don't want to know."

She grinned at him and shrugged. "Okay."

Okay? Just like that? The absolute trust and faith she had in him felt almost as good as making love to her. He didn't understand how she could give him everything. He'd earned none of it, deserved even less. He was going to be a greedy fucking bastard and take everything she would allow for as long as she would.

Someday she'd figure out he wasn't one of the good guys and she'd leave him to save herself. Until then he'd do everything he could to make her as happy as she looked now.

Jett rolled off the bed and stood, shucking his jeans. The warm air from the fireplace felt damn good on his bare skin. He grabbed his cock in his fist and pumped it once, squeezing the head to help him maintain some control. If he wasn't careful he'd blow his load inside of her in only a couple of strokes. She deserved better than that. He wanted to give her his best.

"Do that again." Yvaine smiled drowsily and her words were like a purr.

"This?" He ran his hand up and down his shaft again, keeping his touch light. He didn't need any more stimulation, but he'd do whatever she asked of him.

"Yes. That's really effing sexy."

"You're the one who is fucking sexy. I could come simply from staring at you. What do you want, love? What do you like?"

"Everything you've already done. What do you like?"

"I want to fuck you. I want your legs wrapped around my waist as I thrust into you. I want to feel your cunt tighten and squeeze my cock until neither of us know our names. Tell me you want that. Tell me you want me to fuck you, Yvaine."

She sat up and scooted down to the edge of the bed. "I want that. Ooh, yes. Let's do all of that."

He stepped between her open legs and lifted her up, cupping her ass in his hands. He wanted to lay her out on the plush carpet in front of the fire place and take her there.

"Say it." He loved that she was up for everything he wanted to do to her. She wasn't shy or timid about sex and that was a major turn on.

"Duck me." Her forehead wrinkled and she slapped her hands over her mouth.

Jett laughed and nuzzled her ear. "Duck... you?"

She shook her head and slowly lowered the mask of her fingers. "I mean, funk me. Oh no. Don't do that. Fluck me. Ack."

One of her eyebrows went up and the other down at what was coming out of her mouth. Her hands flew back up to her mouth and she did that squeaking don't-let-it-out laugh.

Either he'd broken her brain with orgasms or... He backed her up against the nearest wall and held her in place with his body. He tugged her hands away from her mouth. Maybe she needed a little incentive. Jett scraped his teeth over the mark of his dragon across her neck and whispered into her ear in a dark and husky tone. "Yvaine. Say fuck."

"Flaaaark." She drew the word out on a long moan and its meaning was clear. Yet, still not quite what he wanted to hear.

"Try God damn it." He pressed his pelvis against hers and notched his cock right at the perfect spot to make her eyes roll back in her head.

"Dog gone it." She groaned each word and wrapped her hands around his neck.

One more try. He pumped against her, sliding the head of his cock across her clit.

Yvaine leaned into him, rocking her hips, giving as good as she got. She licked the shell of his ear and bit down on his earlobe that sent shockwaves straight to his dick.

"Shit." She felt so damn good.

"Schnozbottles," she replied, her voice as sexy as a siren.

What did that even mean? It was so ridiculous it almost wasn't funny. His interest in the subject was waning fast though. He didn't care if she couldn't say fuck as long as she did in fact, fuck him. He was too damn close to taking her here against the wall and he didn't want their first time to be him rutting like an animal. The fireplace and soft carpet were too far away so he turned and laid her back on the bed.

"You're too good for me, Yvaine."

She lifted each of those delectable thighs and rested them on his hips. "Show me how good you are."

Jett pushed a strand of hair out of her face and kissed her forehead, then her cheek, and then her mouth. He pushed his tongue between her lips and slid inside of her tight pussy. She was so wet that it was almost hard not to just thrust his way into her in one hard stroke. That wasn't how good he was. Slowly, centimeter by centimeter he pressed inside of her, savoring every movement, every flutter of her channel around him.

"Holy fuck, Yvaine. You feel so god-damned good." Another gentle thrust of his hips and he was fully seated inside of her. Her body fit perfectly to his.

"Jett." Her eyes were closed and his name was a whimper. She took in a shuddered breath and opened those gorgeous purple eyes, enchanting him with the lust sparkling in them. "More."

For a second he thought he was hurting her. Thank the shadows he wasn't. He withdrew just the tiniest bit and pushed back in, doing that over and over until she was moving her hips in rhythm with his. She was so beautiful, so perfect.

The glow of black light with red sparkles that used to come from her necklace emanated off her skin, lighting up the room. Whatever this particular part of her magic was, it made her even more beautiful to him. Jett lengthened the strokes he took in and out of her wanting so badly for this to be good for her. He almost didn't care if he ever came. He wanted to watch her face flush, her eyes to drift close, and her body to tense as she got closer to exploding again.

He had no words for what he was feeling. He wasn't sure he'd known joy before, but this, being here with Yvaine might be the definition of it. She grabbed his shoulders, panting hard, and dug her nails in. There was no way she could possibly hurt him, the tiny pinpricks that came with her desperation only pushed him higher, wanting more from her.

"Jett. More. Please. I need..." She bit her lip and whimpered.

He could feel her cunt tightening around him with each thrust, but it wasn't going to be enough to push her over the edge. He had to be better. "Don't worry, love. I'll give you everything."

Jett pulled out and in one quick move had her knees up over his shoulders. He drove into her hard, making sure his center beat against her clit.

She threw her head back and cried out. "Yes. Oh gobstoppers, right there. Like that. Don't stop. Holy, yes."

The glow of her magic went from a soft light to bursts, like fireworks into the air around them. "God, you're amazing, Yvaine. Tell me you're close. Let me see you come with my cock inside of you. Come just for me."

She held his face in his hands and stared so deep into his eyes he was sure he was lost deep in her soul. "Come. With. Me. I want to feel you. All of you."

His hips jerked of their own accord, losing his rhythm. Yvaine pulled her to him and kissed him, sucking his tongue into her mouth and groaning. Waves of pleasure hit him directly in the heart. It wasn't the same feeling as when she'd projected her orgasm onto him before. This came from inside of him.

"Jett, I can feel you. I mean, what you're feeling. It's like I'm inside of you. It's amazing."

In that moment, all the darkness inside of him disappeared. That place he kept hidden from the world so that no one could see how broken and worthless he was filled with her magic, her light, her beauty. He wanted nothing more but to be hers forever.

He couldn't say the words, didn't even know if there were any to tell her how he felt. He did his very best to show her with his body. He didn't understand how this magic worked but he projected every sensation, every emotion he had back to her.

Together, in a brilliant explosion of love, pleasure, and magic, their bodies came together, until the tension was too much, and they came together. He poured himself into her and groaned out her name. She gripped his cock tight inside of her, holding his body with hers, taking everything from him and giving him everything in return.

The room went dark. He'd certainly never blacked out from an orgasm before. He blinked trying to clear his vision, but there was nothing wrong with his eyes. Shadow swallowed the room and the only light was the soft glow from Yvaine's eyes. Jett let his wings unfurl and wrapped them around her protectively.

She curled into his body and sighed softly. "That was incredible. Is this the afterglow?"

Jett had no idea what this was, but he reached his senses out and found nothing that put them in any danger. He recognized shadow when he saw it, when he was in it. He'd travelled through shadow with the cursed.

He opened himself up to it and it ebbed and flowed. He commanded it to recede and it did. He invited it back and the room fell into a velvety midnight once again. This manifestation of the darkness had come... from him. It wasn't evil, it wasn't good. This shadow was natural, like wind, water, earth, and fire. Something inside that had been untapped until now. Yvaine and her magic had unleashed a whole new part of him.

Shadow was his element, his domain, the part of nature made especially for him and his dragon.

Hot pins and needles spread from the back of his neck down his arms and he held on tighter to Yvaine.

How had he not known before? It had to be Yvaine. He really needed to find out what kind of supernatural being lived inside of her soft luscious body. He snuggled her closer to him, cradling her with his arms and wings. "You're my afterglow, love."

Very slowly he let the shadows move back to the corners and dance around the firelight. His body and mind rested peacefully in her arms and fell into a blissful sleep. He never slept long and was surprised to see dusk had fallen when he awoke.

That wasn't what brought him out of his slumber. Someone's soft fingers skimmed over his cock, tickling the sensitive spot under his rim. He peeked one eye open to see her transfixed in the exploration of his body. Her touch was softer than feathers and it was driving all the blood from his head straight south.

She made the cutest little gasp when his dick jerked and hardened under her ministrations. Jett wrapped his hand around hers and tightened her grip. "Leaping lizards. I didn't know you were awake. You scared the bjeebers out of me."

He chuckled but it came out strangled because she followed his directions and stroked him in her fist. He licked his lips struggling not to pump his hips. "Christ, you're adorable. You really can't swear. Is this part of your curse?"

Her gaze was transfixed on his cock sliding through her hand. "I don't know. I never noticed before. We weren't allowed to even think the Lord's name in vain, much less say it growing up in the convent."

"But you know what they mean."

"I'm not dumb. I read. How did you think I knew how to sex it up with you? Romance novels, duh."

He was going to have to get himself some of these romance novels. "Hmm. What else did you learn from your books?"

She glanced up at him and the twinkle in her eyes made his heart skip a beat. "There is something I've never done, but would like to try."

"I'm game for pretty much anything you want to do to me, with me, near me." Please let it be something insanely kinky.

The very tip of her little pink tongue darted out between her lips and she lowered her head, kissing the head of his cock. Jett's jaw went completely slack and he coughed like he'd just choked on his own breath. He didn't dare move at all for fear of losing the warmth of her breath and the promise of her mouth on him.

She relentlessly took tiny tastes, licks and nibbles. There was only so much he could stand before he begged her to fuck him with her mouth. He slipped his fingers into her hair. "Yvaine. Put your mouth on me, take me in, and suck my cock. You're killing me with your teasing."

"I don't want to hurt you with my teeth."

Had she really never sucked a cock before? "I swear you will not. Aside from biting my dick off, you can do no wrong."

"Well, what if I--"

A knock sounded at the door and Yvaine jumped back startled. Jett growled. "Go the fuck away we're busy in here."

A female voice called back through the door. "The mistress asked me to bring you food and drinks."

"We're not hungry."

Yvaine pulled the blanket bunched at their feet off the bed

in one giant tug and wrapped it around herself like a giant towel. She bounded toward the door. "I'm starving."

He had sworn to feed her more often. "Fine. Come in."

He didn't bother covering up his own nakedness. Hopefully it would make the person delivering the food go away all the sooner. Yvaine yanked the door open and a woman in a maid's uniform held a tray. But before she could bring it in, Ciara grabbed it up from her and sauntered into the room with it. "Holy First Dragon, Jettison I don't know your middle or last name. Put some ever-loving clothes on. Jakob would pitch a hissy fit if he knew I saw you in all your naked glory."

Jett folded his arms across his chest. "It's not like you didn't know what we were doing in here."

Ciara rolled her eyes and stuck out her tongue at him and crossed the room. She set the tray down on the coffee table near the fireplace. "So what if I did. I thought Yvaine might be hungry."

"I am. Thanks." She plopped down on the couch and grabbed a bunch of grapes and shoved a couple in her mouth. "Who knew nookie worked off so many calories."

Ciara's eyes went wide and she glanced over at Jett blinking. Her face contorted into some awfully weird looks. She was clearly trying to communicate something to him, but he had no idea what. She gave up and and sat down next to Yvaine. "Do you need anything else? A hot bath, some ibuprofen?"

"Nope. I'm good. More than. I'm pretty darn awesome." Yvaine grinned like a loon and Jett fell a little bit more in love with her.

Ciara giggled and curled her feet up under her on the love seat next to Yvaine like she was going to stay for some tea.

Not a chance. Jett was nowhere near done making love to

his mate. Yeah. That's right. His mate. A warmth built in his chest, somewhere around the vicinity of his heart.

His. Mate.

"Enough, Ciara. Thank you for the food and the room. Off you go."

With a snarl and a puff of smoke, Ciara scooted her butt back toward the door. "Okay, okay. I'm going."

"Oh, could I borrow some clothes for the morning. Mine are, well." Yvaine jerked her chin in the direction of the pile of scraps that used to be her clothes.

"Sure. No problem. I'm totally here for whatever you need. Girl talk later, you know, whatever."

Jett shut the door before Ciara was finished talking. The sooner he could get his mate fed and back to bed the better. There was so much more he wanted to do with her before morning. He went to the bed to grab a couple of pillows. Since they were already in front of the fire they might as well try his original on the carpet plan.

He grabbed one and saw a grey smudge on the sheets. He frowned and touched the spot. His fingers came away slightly damp and what he saw wasn't grey, but silver. He'd seen this before. The silvery slime dripping from Yvaine's chest. This was her blood.

"Jett come have a snack, you've got to be hungry too."

He didn't move. He could barely think. He simply stared at his fingers. "Yvaine?"

"What?" She munched on an apple slice.

"Are you a virgin?" It couldn't be. She was... he'd been so...

"Not anymore."

*Y*vaine stretched under the covers and smiled with every part of her body. Then she snuggled up to Jett and drew long, lazy circles over his chest, up his bicep, along his shoulder and traced the scars there. Sometime in the night he'd wrapped them up in his wings again and she loved the seclusion it gave them.

For the first time in as long as she could remember, Yvaine felt like she was in charge of her life. She had a plan. Go to some place on the map she got from Mr. Bohacek called Holyrood in Scotland. Find the unicorn. Break the curse. Once she executed the plan, she'd know who and what she was. Perfect.

Bonus. Assuming it didn't cause too much pain and suffering to some poor unicorn, plan part deux would be to go save Jett's brothers from hell. If the unicorn was going to die or something, they'd find another way. Her heart practically overflowed with hopeful optimism. She'd gone from zero to would be hero overnight. Now if she could get Jett to quit being such a grump and give her some good morning lovin' all would be right with the world.

"Yvaine," he growled. He didn't open his eyes, but tightened his arms around her. "You need your rest."

"Pththth. You're being so sensitive about this. I'm fine. I don't need rest and recovery. I need your big wiener in my vajayjay."

He'd refused to have sex with her again last night after their late-night snack when he figured out she had been a virgin. It took quite a bit of naked teasing to even get him to kiss her. He wouldn't let her get anywhere near his penis. Not with her fingers, not with her hands, and definitely not with--"

"No. I can feel you plotting in that interestingly dirty mind of yours, and the answer is no."

"Why not? You don't have to even do anything. I've always wanted to try reverse cowgirl."

He made a strangled sound and then took a deep breath. "Because."

"That's not a reason. If you're worried about me being on top how about doggy-style."

"I took your innocence, god damn it." He practically shouted the words.

"Oh poo. We did lots of other things together I've never done before, like fight demon batstriches, teleport, fly. It's not a big deal." The second she'd left the convent she'd wanted to do all the things she'd never been allowed to. She'd been too scared to do most of them on her own. Now she had a partner in crime. Sure, sure, losing her virginity was supposed to be some holier than though, life-changing, biblical event. It had been life changing, but not because she wasn't a virgin anymore.

Jett pulled his wings back in and got out of bed. He yanked on his jeans and ran a hand through his hair. "Yes. It is. We don't know what you are and if there are consequences of being with someone like me."

"No. It isn't." She knelt on the edge of the bed and grabbed his hand. He tried to yank it away, but she held tight and pressed his palm to the spot over her heart. "The only part that is a big deal to me is that I did it with you. I can't imagine letting anyone else touch me the way you do."

The shadows in the room elongated and warmed the area around them. She liked that. Made the space feel... like Jett. "The way I want you to touch me now."

"You must be part siren because I absolutely cannot resist you." He twisted the fingers he had pressed over her heart and ran his knuckled down her breast bone and caressed the soft skin on the underside of one nipple turning it hard with the attention.

She leaned into his touch and covered his hand with hers. "I want this. I want you. Touch me, make love to me again."

"I want you so fucking bad I ache with the need. I don't want to hurt you."

Words were not going to convince him. Yvaine grabbed the back of his neck and when he didn't move pulled herself up so they were face to face. She stared deep into his burning eyes, inched so very close and took his bottom lip between her teeth and bit just hard enough to make him hiss with the tiniest nip of pain. That was all it took to get him to throw her back down on the bed and kiss her half senseless with gentle teasing kisses.

"Jett, I like it when you're all hard to my soft. Don't be gentle. Be you."

He responded by burying his face in her neck at scraping

his teeth up and down her dragon mark. He softly whispered, "Mine." He shoved her thighs apart and cupped her mound. His fingers played along her folds, skating over her clit then testing her entrance. "I need you to be dripping wet because I'm going to take you hard, Yvaine. You want me, that's what you're going to get."

Her yes came out as an incoherent jumble of moans and groans. He pulled her juices from her, spreading them, making every inch between her thighs slick. His touch was hot and anything but gentle and she loved it.

"More, Yvaine. Your body needs to beg for mine." He slid two fingers into her and dropped his thumb lower, stroking over the tight ring of muscles there.

If he wanted more, that touch was the way to get it. A shudder shot through her core and her body contracted on the verge of coming. She'd had no idea her bum was good for anything but cushioning the blow when she fell. She was going to have to find some of those extra dirty romance novels and do more research. Or she could just ask Jett to show her.

"I really want you to that some more, but if you don't get inside of me, I'm probably going to die. So do that first. Butt stuff later."

"Put your hands over your head and hold on to the bed." He shoved his jeans down his legs and grabbed his cock in his hand. She was more than ready when he positioned himself between her legs. "Now, Yvaine. Hold on tight."

She scrambled to do as she was told and he slammed into her, filling her so completely. It took him only a minute to set up a punishing pace, pounding into her, fucking her so hard it moved the whole bed. This was so wholly different than the way he'd taken her last night. That had been wonderful and beautiful and special. This, what they were doing now? Was even better.

She stared up at him, loving the dark need in his eyes. Waves of black light swirled around them and every time he pushed into her little red sparks exploded. The magic they were making with their bodies danced around them to a beat shared only between the two of them. Yvaine hardly recognized her own voice when she heard the moans begin. She was turned on by the sound of herself. She was so sexy, not something she'd ever felt or ever thought she would. He made her into a sex goddess.

Jett reached between their bodies and pressed his thumb against her already throbbing clit. He didn't even have to stroke over the bundle of nerve, every drive of his hips back and forth, put a thrilling pressure that sent shudders of desire into her. He growled deep and low, the black light shifting into shadows around him. The dragon inside of him shimmered to the surface and Yvaine saw a glimpse of the wild beast. It was dangerous, damaged, and defiant, demanding with one look that she give all of herself to him.

He claimed he had no soul, but Yvaine was looking right at his. She reached for it with her own and when they touched time stopped, they were the only two beings in the universe, and in the quiet calm before the storm, she fell in love with this glimpse of his true self.

"Yvaine," he cried with a desperate croak, "be mine."

"I am."

Dark and light exploded around them and Jett pushed her over the edge into a blissful throbbing orgasm. He thrust into her twice more until he shook with the power of his own climax and locked their bodies together. Prismic light floated around them and they clung to each other, finding their way back down to earth.

She floated in that lovely place with Jett inside of her, the two of them connected in a deep and intimate way. This was her favorite place to be and she'd stay forever if he'd let her.

"Babe? Yvaine?" There was the slightest edge of worry to the way he said her name.

She couldn't let him think there was anything wrong. Especially since everything was oh, so right. "Hmm?"

"Wow." He pushed a stray lock of hair out of her eyes and she stared up at him with a soft, sloppy feeling. "I think I just won out over food. Ciara knocked and said breakfast is ready."

"Mmm. Breakfast." She could eat, but she didn't want to move. "In a minute."

He tried to pull away from her and she squeezed him tight between her legs. Thunder thighs had to come in handy some time in her life. "Not yet."

He tricked her into releasing him with a long, slow, distracting kiss. "Come on, love. We've got a long journey ahead of us. But I promise to fuck you at least twice more tonight."

Yay.

"Okay, fine, you big bully." She rolled out of the bed but stopped and stared, watching Jett pull his jeans back up. They hadn't even made it past his knees in their hurry. He had one fine toukas. Which reminded her. "But you're doing more of that naughty business you tried earlier."

He ran his hand along the back of his neck, trying to hide his smile from her. "It was all naughty business."

She searched around the floor for her own jeans and took

them toward the en suite bathroom. "You know what I mean. Butt stuff."

"Hell. I've created a monster."

"You know you want to." She waggled her toosh at him.

"You're going to be the death of me."

She hoped she'd be the opposite.

After a quick wash, some creative styling of a small lap blanket off the love seat to make it a wrap that at least covered her boobs and Yvaine really was ready for breakfast. She hoped there was donuts.

Jett didn't bother with his shirt and the way his jeans hung low on his hips almost had her dragging him back to the bedroom. If not for their plans to find the unicorn, she would have. Instead they found Ciara and Jakob in the kitchen. Jakob had a cup of coffee for her, and Ciara had mimosas again. That girl knew how to brunch, yo.

There was a whole spread of eggs and bacon, but Yvaine went straight for the hash browns and yay, donuts. Mmm. Fruity jam filled ones.

Ciara eyed her up and down, but blinked and dipped her head, seemingly satisfied with whatever had her curiosity. Probably the faux shirt. "You feeling okay this morning? I thought you might want some protein after your, hmm, evening activities."

"Thanks, but this will do. I'm vegetarian." She could go for some more of those strawberries they'd had yesterday. Aha, they were on the table already.

Jett frowned at her. "Are you trying to save the world one cow at a time?"

She took a bite of donut and thought about her response. It had never been about saving animals or whatever. Meat just wasn't an option. She swallowed. "Nope, the thought of it makes me want to throw up. I get that there's a whole circle of life, and you can eat whatever you want. Although I might make you brush your teeth after you eat dead animals."

"Did your parents raise you vegetarian?" Ciara asked.

"The nuns were vegan. I've never eaten meat in my whole life." Maybe the only thing she missed about the convent was their garden. Kudos to Ciara and Jakob for not flinching at her mention of being an orphan.

"Never? But bacon is so good." Jakob waved a piece back and forth before popping it whole into his mouth.

She imagined dragons went through quite a bit of pig products. "Blech. I'll stick to the four food groups of fruit, vegetables, grains, and donuts. Thank you very much."

Jett grabbed the little box of strawberries and pushed it over to her. She rewarded him by taking a bite out of one and sucking the juices totally inappropriately. He coughed and stepped behind the island where his lower half was hidden from view.

Jakob had to cover his mouth to keep from spitting out his coffee everywhere. "Ahem. You said you wanted to leave this morning. Do you know where you're headed or how you'll travel. I assume you won't be flying."

"Hard to keep to the air when someone keeps turning me back into a human." Jett made mean eyes at her and took a tearing bite of bacon.

Hmph. She didn't like to fly anyway. "I've got a Eurail pass here somewhere. Do they go to Scotland?"

Jett scoffed. "But it's not yours."

Yvaine shushed him. What a tattletale. She didn't need Ciara thinking she was some sort of common thief. She'd never steal from them. Unless they happen to be walking down the street with their bags hanging open. Then she'd do it so no one else could.

Ciara raised her champagne glass. "How about we just lend you one of our cars?"

"Road trip!" Yvaine had been on the road for months, but mostly hitchhiking or walking. No speed limits meant they'd be across the English Channel in no time. That got them that much closer to making all her dreams come true. Other than getting laid. That was one double checked off the list. "Autobahn here we come."

"You're not driving." Jett was not being very gracious.

Yvaine put her hands on her hips. "Why not? You got to drive last time and we ended up in a steaming pile of junked Boxster and tree."

"Because you don't have a driver's license." His face said something else entirely. 'Your fault' to be exact.

"You don't either." Probably. What did she know? Did they even give licenses to dragons?

"Neither of you are driving. I am." A deep resonating voice boomed into the kitchen area. Standing in the doorway, leaning against the wall like he didn't have a care in the world was a very tall, very blond, golden to the point of almost sparkly, man who was most definitely also a dragon. Yvaine didn't know who he was, but probably he was some sort of dragon royalty. He had that kind of air about him.

Jett stiffened and threw his bacon down on the plate. This must be serious. "Fuck you, Cage. This is none of your business. What the hell are you even doing here?"

Golden boy straightened up too and pointed a finger at Jett. "Jakob called me right after you showed up, bastard. I've been looking for you."

Nope, nope, and no way, Jose. Nobody put her Jett in a

corner. Yvaine stepped in front of Jett and pointed her finger right back at this Cage dude. "Keep your name calling to yourself, buster."

The man's golden eyes sparkled and he gave her a wide grin. "My apologies, miss. I didn't realize our black rogue dragon was under anyone's protection."

She could practically feel Jett bristling behind her so she grabbed one of his arms to keep him in human form. Plus, also she liked touching his muscles. If he could protect her from her enemies, she could do the same. "Don't you forget it. Now, who are you?"

He half bowed like a prince or something. "I am Cage Gylden, the Gold Wyvern and leader of the dragon warriors."

She stuck out her hand to him. The nuns always said you could catch more flies with honey than vinegar. Dragonflies too. "Yvaine."

He held onto her hand a little too long then kissed it instead of shaking it. "Just Yvaine?"

"You want a fancy title? I can make one up. Yvaine de Hythus, pickpocket and Houdini extraordinaire and mate to the Black Rogue Dragon. How was that?" Sounded fancy. She might start introducing herself like that anyway.

"Mate?" Jakob and Cage said together.

"Told ya," Ciara said and topped off everyone's mimosas with champagne, winking at Yvaine when she refilled hers.

Cage tipped his head sideways and glanced at Jett and then at Yvaine's chest. What was with this guy? Were all dragon leaders so, so, pervy? "Hey. Eyes up here, buddy."

His gaze remained exactly where it was, a smidge above boobline. "This isn't another Portia, is it?"

"No." Jett didn't say anything more.

She'd ask him about this other woman later. When they

were alone and she could torture it out of him with kisses, below the belt. Because all's fair in love and war. "I don't care who is driving, let's pack some lunch and snacks and get this show on the road."

"On the road to Geshtianna's new hideout since Jett is the only one who knows where she and my dragons are being held." Cage twirled keys in his hand.

Woman number two she'd be asking Jett about later. "Good try, oh golden one, but unless that chick is in Scotland, she's gonna have to wait. We've got a unicorn to find, beg for some of its blood, and some curses to cure. Let's go."

Despite marching toward the door, no one followed her. Cage picked up a piece of bacon, chewed it, and swallowed before saying anything. "Rogue, your mate says some very strange things. Unicorns? They are a myth."

Screech. Wait, what? "What are you talking about? Of course they exist. Come on. Dragons do, witches do, why wouldn't unicorns?"

Cage examined Yvaine looking at her now like she was not the sharpest hoe in the garden. Snortlaugh. Little did he know. He shrugged and looked to Jakob for confirmation. "They simply don't. Who told you they did? Perhaps someone acting under the influence of Geshtianna or Ereshkigal to lead you farther away from where they are hiding my dragon warriors and Portia."

Yvaine was all ready to defend dear Mr. Bohacek but Jett pulled her to him and kissed her on the top of the head. "Don't worry, love. We will find your unicorn. I believe they are real and are the solution we both need."

Cage rolled his eyes. "Don't be a dumbass."

Yvaine threw a strawberry at the dragon leader's head. "Hey, what did I say about name-calling?"

Golden boy caught the strawberry. "Sorry. I don't want to see you taken advantage of, Yvaine of the pickpockets. No one believes in unicorns but little girls who watch too much My Little Pony."

Jett stared down, that white fire burning there. She sure as hello kitty hoped that was a good sign. He stroked her cheek then turned his fiery gaze on Cage. "Tell that to the First Dragon."

"*I*'m not saying it again, so listen close this time, Goldilocks. Yes, Yvaine and I talked to the First Dragon. He told us to find a unicorn and gave us this map." He left out the part where the First Dragon hadn't spoken to him or even acknowledged his presence. "Yes, I do know it was him and yes I remember every word of the conversation. Quit. Asking. Just. Drive."

Jett turned in the seat to check that Yvaine was still asleep in the second row of the dark green Range Rover. They were almost to The Hague where Cage had used his extensive resources to book them onto a private boat that would shuttle them across the North Sea and drop them almost right at Holyrood Abbey. He'd also arranged for some of Ky Puru's blue dragons to speed them across the water in a fourth the amount of time the boat could cross on its own.

It was nice to have friends in high places. Although, who was he kidding? He and Cage were frenemies at best. Actual enemies at worst. Jett had saved the Gold Wyvern's life a time or two down in hell. His mate's too. Cage owed him. This trip was costing him one of those precious favors. Could they do it without Cage's help? Yes. Did a luxury SUV, back up in the form of gold and blue dragons, weapons, and snacks make it easier on him and Yvaine? Also yes.

"Fine, I get that, jackass." Cage glanced at Yvaine in the backseat too. She'd already popped him on the back of the head for more name calling.

Jett found that hilarious. Cage had assumed the responsibility of AllWyvern, pulling together the four dragon warrior Wyrs under one banner to combine their forces in the fight against the Black Dragon and Ereshkigal. It was likely that nobody even talked back to him these days, much less hit him for being a bully. Except maybe his own mate, Azy. She was full of piss and vinegar that one, with a mouth on her to boot. She'd probably get a kick out of trying to get Yvaine to swear.

Listen to him, practically planning the weekend barbecues and pool parties. Good try, douchepotato. The life of leisure with his mate at his side and little purple-eyed dragon babies running around at his feet was not in the cards for him. Then again, he hadn't thought destiny held a mate for him up her fickle sleeve either.

"Then tell me how the fuck you ended up with a mate, you shardless bastard."

"Hell if I know. She just showed up."

Cage left the most important part of the question hanging in the air. No shard, no soul, no soulmate. Cage knew it better than anyone, since a succubus had once stolen his soul shard to give to Jett. Geshtianna had convinced both him and Portia the scheme would work and they could become mates, like magic.

That had turned out so wrong that they were both still paying for it.

"You're not going to break her heart, are you? She seems sweet. Feisty as shit, but sweet." Cage had been there when Jett had broken Portia's heart.

He'd never loved her. They'd been great in bed together. All along he'd suspected their plan to get him a soul shard would fail. Jett had wondered for a long time whether Geshtianna knew before hand and had set them up to get access to the Gold Dragon Wyr or if she'd really thought shards were transferable.

His father sure had. It's where Jett and Geshtianna had gotten the idea in the first place. The Black Dragon wanted a Wyvern's soul shard and the mate to go along with it. Because with those two pieces of the puzzle locked in place, a dragon came fully into his power. Jett had partially experienced what having Yvaine by his side had done for him. He was stronger, his dragon form bigger, and now he had the shadow on his side.

"I know I don't deserve her, but I will do everything in my power to protect her." They could never fully bond without that exchange of souls. That flaw in fate's plan was Jett's out. He would leave her if he had to, if being with him was going to destroy her.

"Even if it means giving up the battle to defeat the Black Dragon all on your own?" Cage dug into Jett's psyche so easily while expertly navigating them through the streets of the country that used to be his like it was no big deal.

Jett couldn't answer that, which scared the shit out of him. He'd been plotting patricide literally as long as he could remember. The moment he'd become a slightly more than self-aware down in hell, the need to be the one who meted out the retribution for his father's atrocities was all that had pushed him to survive. He knew how to fight the forces of hell better than anyone. Because he was one of them.

That was the only reason Cage was helping him now. The Gold Dragon Wry home been in the Netherlands for hundreds of years. Until hell's forces had razed it to the ground, along with the help of the Queen of the Succubus. He'd made Jett promise, with a bit of prodding from Yvaine, to reveal how to find Geshtianna and her coven. All of Cage's money, technology, and resources, weren't worth squat when it came to the succubus. She knew everything there was to using her resources wisely to keep her hidden. If she didn't want to be found, the dragon warriors wouldn't have a clue where to even begin the search for her.

But Jett did. All he had to do was ask.

"Are we there yet? Is it lunch time? Can we stop and stretch our legs before we get on the boat?" Yvaine sat up in the back seat and yawned. The black t-shirt stretched enticingly across her chest. Jett had sworn when Ciara had given it to her the shirt had been plain. But smack dab in the middle, directly over her heart and the scar from her attack, was a sparkly fucking unicorn. it had to be a sign that she was so obsessed with them.

"We're pulling up to the docks now. You'll have plenty of time to stretch your legs while Jett tells me where to find Geshtianna and my missing dragons," Cage replied.

She yawned again and took out a bag of snack-sized carrots from the cooler Ciara had packed for them. "Oh good."

"Nope, it's oh shit, I'm afraid." Cage slammed on the breaks and stared out the front window. Twenty-five meters in front of them was a being that should not be there.

Yvaine pointed with her carrot. "What the flip is that?"

Jett and Cage said the word simultaneously. "Annunaki."

What was she doing here? Either she was with Geshtianna and this was a fucking ambush, or she'd used her connection to Jett. Either spelled danger with a capital Black Dragon. He scanned the area searching for shadows that shouldn't be there, or that were too big, too dark. He pushed a few back for good measure.

"Annie who now?"

The sound of a sword being pulled from its sheath filled the car. Cage moved slowly and deliberately, preparing for battle. "One of the seven judges of the underworld and Ereshkigal's personal guard. But what the fuck it's doing here, I don't know. They aren't supposed to be able to leave hell."

Jett opened his senses to the Annunaki demon and was struck by a familiar scent. Here in the land of the living, she didn't smell the same as in the underworld. That's why he hadn't recognized her. He did now. She'd been in the town near the Green Wyvern's villa, she'd been at the field where they'd crashed the car, she'd been on the rooftops, she'd been at the pub.

She was the creature hunting Yvaine.

But why? A thousand and one razor sharp fears struck him directly in the gut. She would be here if she sensed the changes Yvaine had caused in Jett, in his power. What the Annunaki knew, Ereshkigal knew. What the Black Witch knew, the Black Dragon could use to incapacitate Jett. They had sent her after Yvaine.

The Annunaki drifted closer, her robes flowing around her to hide the darkness beneath the clothing. Her arm raised up and she pointed a bony finger at Yvaine.

"Why is it pointing it's finger at me? I do not like that. Not even a little bit." She pointed her finger back and shook it. Jett grabbed her arm and pushed it down.

Cage shoved the driver's side door open and held his golden sword aloft in front of him. Jett and Cage had fought the Annunaki before. They'd lost. The only reason they were still alive was because of Azy and Fallyn, the Black Dragon's daughter. There wasn't anyone here to save them now. "Take your mate and go, Jett. Find the unicorn."

Jett got out of the car and joined the Gold Dragon. He didn't have a fancy weapon like Cage, but he did have the element of shadow surprise. "You can't fight the Annunaki alone. She will kill you and you still owe me a damned favor."

Not to mention if the leader of the dragon warriors was killed while helping Jett and Yvaine, the rest of the dragon warriors wouldn't be inclined to ally with him again. He did not need more enemies. He'd thought he had to fight his battles on his own. He never even considered asking for help. Until now.

"Don't you worry your pretty little head over me. I'm like a Girl Scout. Always prepared." Cage punched at the watch on his wrist. "Move in."

Two more SUVs, big black ones like in the movies, screeched in from opposite sides. The doors popped open and the dragon muscle squad swarmed out like it was a clown car. Jett didn't recognize any of them personally, but he inherently knew they represented every Wyr. The two reds shifted immediately and didn't take their eyes off the Annunaki. Which was probably good because Jett was only about a step above pond scum to them.

A shimmer of sunshine signaled Cage's shift into his dragon form. The sword shifted with him and became a deadly metal spike in his tail. *Don't disappear on me this time, rogue. The fate of my children lies with you.*

No pressure there. The fate of the entire fucking world

pressed down on Jett. Save his brethren, defeat the Black Dragon, keep Yvaine safe, don't let the dragon babies get screwed in the fight between good and evil. He wasn't strong enough to bare it, not without Yvaine and the dragon warriors. Damn it. He needed them as much as they needed him. Duck a ducking duck.

If he stayed he could use his new control over shadow to help them capture her. He couldn't stand the thought of letting her get anywhere even close to Yvaine though. Yvaine would never even see an entrance to hell of he could help it. Fuck. He couldn't risk it. The dragon warriors had this under control. Sort of. His priority had to be her and getting to the unicorn. If Cage died, Jett would spend the rest of his days making sure Azy and the babies were taken care of. If Yvaine died, he would spend those same days burning down the world. "Yvaine, get out of the car very slowly. Don't make any sudden moves that will draw its attention back to you."

She slid out of the back seat and crept over to him. "Jett? Why is that thing here? Is it after you? I can try to use my disappearing act and get us out of here. Just trap us somewhere, like one of those shipping containers. Oh. But I don't know if I can transport all of the dragons too. I have better control over it now, but I think I can only do you and me."

"No, love. If you were going to turn me into dragon form, this would be a good time." He kept his voice cool and calm for her. "We cannot stay and fight, and these dragon warriors would be pretty pissed if you zapped them all away to safety. They were born and bred to fight demons. You were born to find a unicorn. So let's go do that."

Yvaine glanced over at the dragons circling the Annunaki. She barely noticed their presence. She only had eyes for Yvaine. "Crudmuffins. Okay."

She closed her eyes and wrinkled up her nose and fore-head. Nothing happened. Jett had a feeling that might happen. More than his newfound affinity for controlling the shadow had changed inside of him when he'd claimed her.

One more try. "Come on, babe. Don't make me tell you there's a spider on your shoulder."

"Ack." She peeked one eye open. "There is not."

The Annunaki moved forward and the dragon warriors closed their circle. It wouldn't be long until the demon noticed them and decided to kick their asses. "Babe. Try again."

She scrunched up her face tighter and clenched her fists so tight her arms shook. "I am trying. Nothing's happening."

Cage struck at the demon but only to hold her attack back. From behind her more Gold dragons appeared, flying in from nearby rooftops. They were joined by a handful of blue dragons who floated right up out of the water. They sprayed the Annunaki with their icy breath, freezing her in place. She burst out of the trap almost immediately. The attack hadn't broken her line of sight on Yvaine.

Yvaine grabbed his arm. "I can't change you. I swear I'm scared out of my ever-loving mind right now and you're still you. What are we going to do?"

Jett reached inside of himself, searching for the touch of magic that had always allowed him to shift from man to dragon and back again. It was there, stronger than ever before. Stronger, yet different. The magic was... more a part of him and less some sort of spell he had access to. No wonder he missed it. He let the dragon explode from him and flapped his wings, filling the area underneath them with shadow. He shaped the darkness into a sphere and pushed it at the Annunaki. She who had raised him, who had saved him from Ereshkigal's curse, and who had helped him escape from hell.

He roared out a warning.

Stay away from her, mother.

The Annunaki finally took notice of him, raised her arm and shoved a burst of shadow at him. It knocked him back, pushing him away from Yvaine and the oncoming battle for her. She was within striking distance of Yvaine and Jett had to play the card he'd been holding close to the vest. *Cage, I can command the shadow. I will trap her in path that repeats back on itself. If you surround that with your sunlight, she will not be able to escape, either to hell or to follow me and Yvaine.*

Cage looked at Jett surprised. Shadow was an element outside of the realm of dragon warriors' scope of powers. Only those born of hell would understand. Cage was the only one who might get it. His element was sky, which encompassed sun. Light and Dark. Heaven and Hell. Where there was one, there must be the other.

Jett gathered the shadow and thrust it at the Annunaki. She would be forced to wander in a figure eight until someone broke the shadow path. Rays from the sun shot down from the sky, obeying the command of the AllWyvern. *Thank you, brother. Now go.*

Brother?

Jett. Go.

Don't kill her. She's your key to finding Geshtianna. The Succubus Queen and her brother are bound to Ereshkigal as her servants. The Annunaki are their keepers. Jett didn't wait to see if the dragon warriors were smart enough to figure out how to get the Annunaki to give them Geshtianna or her location. He grabbed Yvaine into his talons, cupping her body gently, but securely in his claws and flew up and over the North Sea.

"Oh my gosh, holy cannolis, Bob's your uncle. Don't you dare drop me, Jett. Ahhhhh. Please don't turn back into a human either." Yvaine was freaking out. The fear in her psyche about being off the ground punched at him with the force of a jackhammer. She really did not like to fly.

She had nothing to fear from him. He would protect her. *Shh, love. You're safe.*

"What if I accidentally touch you and you drop me into the ocean. I can't swim very well."

Hold on to me as tight as you like. I won't shift back until we are safely on land again.

"Are you sure? I really don't want to swim with the sharks."

There aren't any sharks in the North Sea.

"Kraken?"

No, they live in the Greek isles. You're safe, love. I swear it. On my life. You're safe with me.

It took them only minutes to cross the water. Cage must have sent one of his gold's to push them along with the wind because he flew faster than he ever had. The shoreline came into view and Jett swooped down toward a beach. They should be close to where the map was directing them if he landed there. Flying over the city of Edinburg at dusk would have the humans up in arms. They came in very low over the water, his talons skimming over the water. If anyone saw them like this perhaps they'd think he was some sort of a speedboat.

"Mommy, mommy. Look at that lady with a dragon."

Or perhaps not. Jett gently set Yvaine down in the sand next to a broken down looking wooden sea wall and shifted back to his human form. Yvaine waved at the little boy who'd called them out. The mother didn't seem to take notice of them. They walked up the beach toward the street and Yvaine got out the map.

"I think we're right about here at Portobello beach. Mmm. Portobello burger sounds good. Fighting demons and flying over death defying waters makes me hungry." She scanned the street across from where they were standing and pointed to a fish and chips shop. "Ooh. Get me some fried potatoey goodness and I'll love you forever. Come on."

The fact that she wasn't even bothered that they'd encountered a demon who'd been hunting her for at least days, flown across the ocean, which seemed to be a big phobia for her, and were in yet another foreign country made Jett fall in love with her that little bit more. "If all it takes is potatoes to get you to love me, I'll buy you a whole farm."

She stood on her tiptoes and kissed his cheek. "Thanks. Now feed me."

They crossed the street, ordered food and he watched her eat and pour over the map. He could do this for hours. This was peaceful perfection and Jett's chest filled with such a sense of longing for a life like this with her that he physically ached. What if he didn't battle the Black Dragon? What if they left the rest of the world behind and stayed far away from demons and dragons forever? Would she do that with him?

"Yvaine."

"Hmm?" She popped another bite into her mouth and traced the path she wanted them to take to Holyrood Abbey.

"I love you."

She stopped mid-chew and looked up from her map. She swallowed and licked her lips. "You do?"

"Yes."

The smile that formed from her lips spread to her eyes,

across her face, and through her whole body. She took his breath away and he'd gladly give it to her.

"I thought you'd think I was super weird if I told you the same thing. I mean, it's only been like two days. But I love you a lot. Like really, really a lot."

The room around them fell quiet, into an unnatural hush. "Aww. Isn't that sweet. Jett's in love so he can't be bothered to break the curse on his brothers like he promised them he would. Adorable."

Jett's dragon shimmered to the surface and his senses reached the speaker before his eyes found him. Standing behind them in the doorway of the shop was a man who was also a dragon.

A black dragon.

A demon dragon. The one who had killed Yvaine.

BROTHERS, OH BROTHER

"Yvaine, get behind me." Jett shoved the stool he was sitting on over and stood in front of her. The shimmer of black light that preceded his shift into dragon form swirled around him. She placed her hand on his back making sure he knew she was there and safe for the time being. He growled low in his throat. "What spell has Ereshkigal cast on you brother? If you think you can touch Yvaine, I will send you back to hell myself."

The other people who had been in the shop with them were long gone, smart enough to know trouble when they saw it. The sun had set outside and the street was dark. Too dark. The shadows inside the shop grew and Yvaine clung closer to Jett. She was tired of all the fighting, of having to battle another creature every other minute.

Was this the kind of life Jett led on a daily basis? She had to put a stop to it if it was. He couldn't live a real life this way. She slipped out from behind Jett, under his arm when he tried to stop her and held out her hand to the other man. "Hi. I'm Yvaine. I don't really know how everything works here in the paranormal world, I'm kind of new, but I think you're maybe my new brother-in-law."

The man hissed and stepped back from her. Jett yanked her away. "Don't touch him. He tried to kill you."

"When? No, he's too good looking to be a killer. Besides he's your brother, so there has to be some good in him." She understood there was good and evil in this world, but she had a hard time believing that most creatures would choose to harm, maim, and kill as Jett and the other dragon warriors had described that the demon dragons did. Besides. Jett thought he could somehow save them. If it was a curse that kept them from being their true selves, it wasn't their fault if they'd had to be creepy minions to the baddies of hell.

"Yesterday," he snapped. "I cannot vouch for his actions if he's under a dark spell and being controlled by Ereshkigal or the Black Dragon. We need to get you out of here before he alerts the Annunaki."

"I'm no longer connected to them. I can however still feel our brethren being tortured by the curse. The one you promised us you would break. You've betrayed us all for her, haven't you?" The man bared his teeth at Yvaine and his eyes went from black to red. A fire similar to Jett's burned in his pupils.

Yikes. Except those fires were angry and they were directed at her. She didn't understand why he had his mad on or why he thought Jett had betrayed him. Pretty much from the beginning Jett had made it clear his goal was to save his brothers. The only time he'd relented even a little was for sexy times. If this guy knew how awesome doing the deed was, he wouldn't hold that against Jett, surely.

"I have not betrayed you. She's the key to breaking the

curse. She will lead us to a unicorn and it's blood will free all the demon dragons under Ereshkigal's spell."

"Why do we need unicorn's blood, when we have hers? Let us rend her limb from limb and feed her to any demon dragon who wants free of the demon bond. Then together we can rise up and overthrow the AllFather."

Umm. How about they didn't do that. Yvaine really didn't want to sacrifice something as cool as a unicorn. She was still crossing her fingers they would only need a few drops and the creature would be all happy to give it to them since it could help save the world and all.

"I will never sacrifice her. We do not even know what kind of being she is or if her contact with you is what broke the spell. The First Dragon himself has given us the means to find the unicorn. He confirmed its blood will break any curse. Our brethren need not wait much longer for the revolution."

"We have waited long enough. You can go in search of something none of us even know exists or not. I will take the girl. Her body alone will break the curse for at least a dozen more demon dragon. Maybe more. We will have to see how much of her blood each needs. I held her heart in my hands. Hopefully that was more than enough."

"Do. Not. Touch. Her."

The demon dragon man didn't listen. Nope. He shifted into a big black dragon that filled the entire tiny fish and chips shop with its giant butt.

Jett also shifted and his body broke the wall behind him. They were going to be in so much trouble. Yvaine could already hear the neener-neener of sirens headed their way.

"Jett, sit on me."

Run, love. Run to the abbey. Find the unicorn.

"Sit on me right now. I'll be trapped and we'll zap out of here. Then you don't have to fight your brother."

You're not going anywhere, little beast. The other dragon swiped at her with its claws and she avoided him by taking a dive toward the wall. She clocked her head on the broken bricks and little birdies and stars floated around her head.

That made Jett fricking explode. Or maybe that was all in her head because she suddenly couldn't see him or the other dragon anymore. The bricks and tables and chairs disappeared and instead of sitting on the tile floor of the shop, she found herself in the grass outside some sort of castle mansion looking building.

Aw, fudge. She'd Houdini'd without Jett.

She pushed herself off the ground and tried to see if she could hear him in her head. *Jett?*

Nothing but the insects chirping. Fine. She'd just had to figure out where she was and get back to the beach. They hadn't gone more than a couple of miles the last time she'd done this, so she was hoping the same would be true again. She pulled the map out of the pocket of her pants and scanned for a castle. Aha. There was one. Palace of Holyroodhouse.

Oh. A shiver raised the hair on the back of her neck and skated down her arms. The Holyrood Abbey was just on the other side of the palace. That was where Mr. Bohacek had indicated on the map that she should go to find the unicorn. She was no more than two minutes away from finding it. She could go, ask it nicely for a couple drips of blood, and know who she was, what she was.

Would she remember who her family was too? What had happened to her or them or both that had landed her in an orphanage? Maybe the unicorn would know. Did unicorn's talk? Dragons did, so possibly.

But what if this was a once in a lifetime kind of a deal. She should go back and get Jett so they could also ask for some blood to break the curse on his brothers. Jett hadn't told her much, only that he planned to save them. But from what the angry demon dragon dude had said, cursed life was literally hell.

Finding the unicorn now on her own was selfish. She'd wanted to know her whole life why no one was there for her, and deep down, why no one had loved her. That wasn't the same level of horribleness as being enslaved to a witch and a king of hell dragon. She could wait. The beach was only maybe an hour walk away. Probably ten minutes if she could find a cab. She would go back and find Jett, tell his brother she knew where the unicorn was and come back.

Maybe just a quick peek at the abbey first to make sure she knew what she was talking about. No going in and definitely no looking for unicorns. She jogged through the grass of the small park that surrounded the palace and got the strangest sense of deja vu. She was sure that she'd recognize what lay beyond the next corner. She'd run through this park before. Growing up.

Yes, the grass, the trees, the flowers. They were all familiar. This was the park outside of her orphanage. There wouldn't be an abbey around the corner, it was an old church that had been converted by the nuns into an orphanage. She'd grown up in that church building. But how could it be here? She didn't remember anything about the city of Edinburg, or even having ever been to Scotland before, much less having grown up here.

Yvaine pushed the muscles in her legs to take her faster, to cross the park and see the church for herself. She sprinted through a copse of trees and down a sand and gravel path.

The edge of the palace wall took a sharp turn and so did she. There, there was the church. It's arched windows and stone facade glowed in the moonlight. But there was something wrong. The outbuildings were gone, only stone outlines in their places. The chapel had no roof. Everything she'd known was in ruins.

She went toward the front where the big wooden doors should be, the feeling of rocks in her stomach grew with each step. She stopped a few feet in front of the church. A blue box stood to the left of the main entryway displaying some sort of tourist information. How could this be? She'd been here only a few months ago. She was sure of it.

Everything was wrong.

"Hello, Yvaine." A woman in long black robes and her head covered stood just inside the crumbling archway.

"Mother Superior?" The woman who Yvaine was sure had hated her as a child simply could not be standing here. She must have hit her head a lot harder than she thought. None of this could be real.

"Open your eyes, child. I think you can see me better than that now."

Yvaine blinked, but still the nun stood there. "I don't understand."

She waved Yvaine toward her. "You should have stayed with us. Then you would still be innocent and wouldn't have to try to understand any of this. You could be safe in our care, just as you mother wanted you to be."

"My mother?" Not once in all the years she'd spent in the orphanage, the countless times she'd been chastised and disciplined by the Mother Superior, the countless nights she'd cried herself to sleep wondering if there was anyone in this entire world who had ever cared about her had anyone ever said anything about her mother. She'd wondered for a long time if it was possible she didn't even have one.

"Come, Yvaine." She sounded a little impatient. "I didn't think we'd see you again. This will give me a chance to explain and let you decide your own fate. If that's even possible anymore."

Choose her own fate. She wished Jett were here now. She would choose him. The unicorn hadn't mysteriously appeared, there was still time to go back to the beach and look for him. She wanted his strength, his love to help her figure out what to do. Without knowing who and what she was she'd be going to him as only a part of herself.

He'd given everything to her. She owed him the same. Yvaine stepped toward the Mother Superior and just as she crossed the threshold of church she heard Jett call her name.

Yvai--

The sound of his voice was cut off and the world around her shifted, changed into something from a dream. Night changed back into day, darkness into a soft light. The ruins of the church were restored, not to stone but to the branches of great big trees that formed a domed canopy. The tinkling sound of children singing somewhere in the forest echoed off the leaves. A cool breeze drifted through her hair where the air should be still and the babbling of a clear brook called to her to take a long quenching drink.

She lowered her head to sip from the water and caught her reflection in a puddle near the grassy bank. Except that could be her. She skittered back and almost fell over her own feet.

Hooves.

She opened her mouth to ask what in the world was going on but the words came out as a soft whinny.

"Shh, shh, shh. Calm yourself, Yvaine. Your body already

remembers who you are, your mind will catch up in a moment. Use your mind to speak, I'll hear you just fine." The voice was that of Mother Superior, but the face and form were not.

Who are you and what is this place? Whoa. Was that her voice?

The woman, fairy, person, thing smiled at her as if to say good job on remembering how to talk. "This is *Sìthean,* the otherworld, your home. I am Cait of the *Sìth.*"

This isn't my home. Although, she did have to admit if felt familiar, comfortable even.

"Ahh, you're right. It was your home. Fate has taken you to a new realm and I fear you're going to stay there with your *brollachan,* aren't you?"

My who? Do you mean Jett? Can you please explain what is going on here?

"Always so impatient. Fine, yes. Maybe if you'd known all along, you wouldn't have been tempted into leaving by that sneaky goddess."

I don't remember any goddess. I don't have a freaking clue what you're on about. Just start at the beginning and when you get to the end, stop.

"A long time ago, in a--"

Wait, skip ahead to the bit about me.

"You're too sassy for your own good, Yvaine. Blah, blah, blah, your mother was dying and asked the *Sìth* to hide you in the otherworld. She didn't want you to suffer the same fate as she."

Wait, back up a smidge. What was my mother's name and why was she dying?

"Your mother very special. The only one of her kind. In the human world she went by the name Margaret de Hythus, but in ours we called her *aon-adharcach*. She had quite the torrid affair with William the Lion, King of Scots. There's been many a tale told of them, but most get it wrong. I am rather fond of the one by that Lewis Carrol fellow. Except your parents weren't fighting over the crown, they were fighting for the Scots to keep it."

But Scotland doesn't have a king.

"It did in the 12th century when you were born and England was trying to conquer the world. Where do you think the Lion got the idea for the royal crest? His love for your mother became part of the national identity of the Scots. You practically tripped over a statue of her at their silly palace out there."

Huh. Yvaine was pretty much out of shock and surprise. She had about a million and one questions but wanted to get back to the real world and Jett to tell him all that she'd discovered. *Okay. So I'm also princess. Great, I'll pop right out the shops and get a tiara. Let's skip ahead a few hundred years. Like about nine-hundred should do it.*

"As you wish." The *sìth* thought for a minute. "Then the goddess showed up, and even though we told her she didn't belong in our realm, she insisted on asking if you wouldn't like to go on an adventure. Something about needing a match for the *brollachan* bastard. None of us could talk you out of it. She planted a story in your head about growing up in an orphanage and plopped you right into the middle of the war between her children, the dragon warriors and the *slaugh*."

I can help turn the tide of their war, can't I?

"Yes, so like your mother. Are you prepared for cost?"

It didn't matter. If she could save Jett's brothers and end his suffering over their fates, she would sacrifice almost anything. *I have to get back. How do I return? Oh, geez. Now that I know what I am, will I still look like this? Jett won't recognize me."*

"No, in their world, you will always appear as the maiden. Only here in Sìthean do you take your true form. Inside you are one in the same. There are so many who spend their entire lives hunting you. But your abilities are for your own survival and can't be used for the gain of others. No one, man, beast, or otherwise will benefit from you gifts unless they are freely given by you."

That was an interesting insight that nobody had thought to mention. Maybe they didn't know. Yvaine understood exactly what she had to do. What she freely wanted to do. She trotted back toward the front of the forest chapel. Hopefully Jett would still be there waiting for her.

"Yvaine, be careful. Like your mother before you, you are the only one of your kind and will be until you have a daughter of your own. She will become as you are when you die. There can only be one. But if you die without any progeny, your line, your magic, will be lost to their world and ours forever."

Gosh. She and Jett needed to get busy having babies. A real hardship that would be. *Thank you, for everything. I'm sorry I thought you were a mean old nun.*

Cait laughed and the ground shook. No. Cait wasn't laughing any more. The soft light of the otherworld fritzed like a bad TV and leaves fell from the trees. "Oh no. They've brought their war here. That stupid *slaugh*. They'll destroy our world yet. I'll close the veil between the two. We've survived their war before, we'll do it again. You could stay here and be safe."

Thanks, but you know I can't.

Cait bowed her head and the doorway between the otherworld and Scotland opened. Yvaine slipped through and into the battle. A burst of flame lit up the sky on the hill just the other side of the trees. The battle seemed to be concentrated there and she had a feeling that was where she would find Jett and a whole lot of trouble. She reached inside of herself, found the magic that she'd used to pass through the veil, what she'd thought was her invisibility power, and slipped through the tiniest crack between the two worlds. This time she could see where she was and where she was going. The *Sìthean* coexisted alongside the human world. A few steps went a whole lot farther in *Sìthean* though. In a second she stood on the hillside a half a mile away.

Jett's brother, the black dragon formerly known as Batstrich Boy was hunkered down, blowing a steady rapid steam of fire bombs. She followed their airborne path toward the enemy and found that stupid big Black Dragon batting them away with ease. The brother's scaly hide was torn and bleeding and he looked ready to collapse, but pushed himself to defend something or someone behind him.

The Black Dragon whipped its tail, which was on fire at one end, around, catching the brother on the jaw and knocking him backward a good twenty feet. Yvaine finally caught a glimpse at what brother black dragon was defending.

On the ground in a pile of pain and suffering lay Jett, bleeding on the ground and directly in the path of the Black Dragon's next fire tail attack.

SACRIFICE

*H*is Yvaine was alive and he was dying.

If he didn't get his sorry ass up and fend off his father's attack, she would be dying along with him.

Come on. This was the pivotal moment in his entire existence, the battle he'd been waiting for, and he couldn't get his worthless body to obey his commands. He was injured yes, but not so much that he couldn't fight. There was something else wrong. It was as if he were under Ereshkigal's curse again.

"Jett, look out." Yvaine screamed and ran toward him. She pointed her finger at the Black Dragon and shouted at him. "You leave him alone, you dead-beat dad, or you'll pay for everything you've ever done to him and his brothers. I swear it."

Fuck, no. He tried to tell her to run away, to use her powers to hide, to get as far away from here as she could. His mind wouldn't work. With all of the strength he had remaining, he pushed himself up and into the path of the Black Dragon's fire whip. He would take the hit to save her, but what would happen after that?

Brother, please. Protect Yvaine. He and his newly freed black dragon brother hadn't solved their differences. He was still angry that Jett had not come back to free them all. He felt they'd suffered long enough and Jett should have gotten any out that he could instead of trying to start a revolution. The cursed demon dragons didn't care if the AllFather was defeated, they only wanted their freedom. Jett had only forestalled his brother's attack by swearing that if they didn't find the unicorn, he would call in all of his favors with his new allies, the Wyverns to stop the fighting and killing of demon dragons and rescue them from hell instead.

That was never going to happen. It was every dragon warrior's duty in life to hunt and kill his brethren. They didn't understand or care that his kind were cursed and forced into slavery. But the promised lie gave him more time. He needed that damn unicorn.

Now his time was running out. *Take her to the Gold Wyvern, he will protect her.*

He's not taking her anywhere, boy. She restored your forsaken soul, now she will do the same for me. The Black Dragon pulled his whip back at the last second and lifted into the air. He dove for Yvaine reaching out for her with his claws. *You're mine now, little savior.*

Was that what his father thought? That Yvaine had given him a soul? Could that be true? She had told him she would share her own with him. Jett hadn't thought that was possible. She had filled him up with her trust. When he'd claimed her he'd been given a new power, become stronger. When he'd allowed himself to admit that his feeling for her were more than lust, he'd found a new peace inside. Her love had done all of that.

If his father thought he could take any of that away from him and use if for himself, he didn't understand how the heart's true power. He couldn't take a soul, shard or the whole thing. It had to be given. Given in exchange for the same. Jett may not have had a piece of his soul to give to Yvaine, but he'd given her everything else of himself.

There was no way he could let the Black Dragon ever touch her. *Yvaine. Please, love. You have to get away.*

"Not without you." She slipped in and out of his vision, avoiding the Black Dragon's attempts to snatch her like a ninja. Gods she was amazing. Wherever she'd been, whatever she'd learned, took her to a level so far beyond his comprehension, it had to be the realization of her true self. "Where you go, I go."

Her words infuriated the Black Dragon and he roared into the sky. His anger, and Yvaine's devotion restored some of Jett's strength. Her mere presence was breaking the new curse on his mind and body. He staggered to his feet and extended his wings. *You'll never take her, Kur-Jara. She is mine.*

And he was hers.

Don't worry. I will take very good care of your little whore. I will bury myself so deep inside of her she won't even remember your name. The Black Dragon blew a heavy stream of fire at him and his brother. They would both be fried to a crisp. Jett used his own power over the shadow to open a path under his brother, who fell through and disappeared almost immediately. It was the only way to save him.

Holy shit. The shadow was the way to save Yvaine and himself too.

He couldn't.

The shadow was a fast track ticket to hell. If he took her with him into the darkness they he would be subjecting her to Ereshkigal's domain. Her pure beautiful bright soul would be irreparably damaged by the taint of evil. If they even survived down there. The cursed demon dragons lurked in the shadows. He'd made them wait too long. They would make it nearly impossible to leave again, not without freeing his brethren too. Without the unicorn's blood, they would be stuck.

But she would be alive. In Hell.

It was the worst idea ever. He'd sworn she would never see the darkness of hell. There had to be another way to escape. She wouldn't use her own powers to leave without him. Unless he wasn't here for her to worry about. She would go if he was dead. Fuck. It would only take one shot. Let his father's fire strike the lethal blow. It would be easy enough to taunt the bastard into it.

But she would be alive.

With half a soul.

She'd literally shared her soul with him. If he died what would happen to her? The power inside of him, the part she had awakened burned with a fire hotter than the center of the Earth, burning him from the inside out. It was a harsh warning. Jett had no doubt whatsoever that if she died, he would too. They were bonded together, forever. Mates for life.

Hold still, you little bitch. I won't hurt you. Much.

Yvaine slipped through the Black Dragon's grasp again and when she reappeared she was right on top of Jett. She barreled into him, slid underneath his armored dragon's belly, and rolled out under his tail. She touched a hand to a wound on his back leg and it healed almost instantly. "There you go. Can you fly? Let's get the dell out of hodge."

Jett snagged her in his talons and gave all his energy to his wings, hoping for the smallest chance that they could fly away. The gold dragons may still be in the skies over the North Sea and if they could just make it that far, they could alert Cage. Who may or may not send a squadron of dragon warriors to battle the Black Dragon. The King of Hell wasn't the top of the priority list for the AllWyvern anymore. His children and Ereshkigal's claim for them had become more important.

If the Black Dragon was going down, Jett would have to be the one to do it. It was his destiny.

Fly away to fight another day, sacrifice himself to save Yvaine with no guarantees she could escape, or take them both down to hell with the chance that his brothers would kill her to gain their freedom. An impossible decision that was suddenly taken out of Jett's hands. He didn't get a chance to lift off the ground with Yvaine. A searing fire hit his left wing and it snapped, breaking at the joint. He faltered under the pain and lost his grip on Yvaine.

You're both mine now. The Black Dragon shot a fireball the size of a pick-up truck at Jett's head and reached out his claws to snatch Yvaine up. Jett called up the shadow with all of his might. He roared into the night sky, opening a crack between hell and earth, letting the shadows that dwelled there to swell and pour into the land. Surrounded by the darkness, together they fell fast and hard into the heat of hell. Jett grabbed Yvaine to him and encircled her in the clasp of his wings. They landed in a dark cave that smelled of fire and brimstone. All the air knocked out of his lungs when he hit the stone, and he had to swallow a grunt of pain when his broken wing snapped again. The only thing keeping him conscious was his need to make sure Yvaine was okay.

Love, are you okay? He reached out his senses and found her shining soul in the darkness like a brightly burning candle in the night. He'd been worried that just passing through the shadow would harm her. She was tougher than he gave her credit for. He would do well to remember that.

She patted his chest and leaned her forehead against him, breathing harshly. "Yeah, but I've got bits of rocks in places that the sun don't shine. Where are we?"

The scraping voice of the crone, Queen of the underworld, answered for him. "Welcome home, dragonling. We've been waiting for you."

Ereshkigal waved her hand, closing the portal of shadow to the Earthly plane above and cut off the Black Dragon's route to follow. Along with her command of the realm came the horde of demon dragons under her control, the cursed ones. She'd been busy with her coup over the Black Dragon. Behind them, her personal guard showed him in no uncertain terms, they were here to made sure he and Yvaine didn't go anywhere. All the Annunaki, except his own mother, encircled Jett and Yvaine. This was no escape. He'd brought them straight into a trap.

"Hand over the girl and you can join your brethren again. I cannot let her live and break any more of my spells." Ereshkigal waved her hand and the Annunaki tightened their circle.

Jett growled at them and shot a warning stream of fire over their heads. *Not a chance, witch. You cannot just give her to the Black Dragon. I won't let you and it wouldn't matter. She cannot redeem his soul the way he thinks she can.*

"Stupid boy. Your father is a lost cause. He is not worth the effort I took to restore his powers. He cannot reclaim his past, his birthright. The fool does not see that Inanna must pay for what she has done." The witch shook with anger. "If she is not held accountable for her crimes she will continue to wreak havoc on all our realms. She has gotten away with her selfishness long enough."

Yvaine clung to him, still wrapped in his wings. "Whoa. She is pissed at this Inanna person. We should not get in the middle of their girl fight."

Too late.

"I had such high hopes for you when I released you from the spell. I thought if I gave you a taste of freedom, you'd see the realities of this war." Ereshkigal signaled to the cursed demon dragons around them and they, unafraid of Jett's fire moved in closer, hissing and growling. Their eyes burned with the fury of hell. He knew it well, but it had never been directed at him. Not good.

Hatred for the Black Witch ignited a renewed need in Jett to raze hell and end the reign of terror over him and his kind. She had broken her own curse over him. He'd always assumed his mother had found a way to do that, to set him free. Even in his freedom, he'd been a pawn to this witch. No more. He would find a way that never again would her bidding be done by him or his cursed brothers.

She waved a hand and three demon dragons advanced on him. They stalked toward him, spotting the weakness in his stance. They hadn't yet spotted Yvaine, but they would know by her scent that she was here. He also saw in their eyes that they were reticent to do the witch's bidding. They stopped only inches from him, and he didn't know if it was of their own will or if the witch had them all exactly where she wanted them.

"Geshtianna was supposed to guide you, not corrupt you with her own agenda. If I hadn't blocked you from communi-

cating with the demon dragons you might have ruined everything. She will pay for her betrayal of me as well. If you don't
want to join her in her six months of torture by my Annunaki,
you'll do as you're told. Give me the girl."

Never. My brethren and I will overcome your hold. He was
talking out his ass at the moment, stalling for time until he
could figure out how to get Yvaine to safety. But every word
was a promise. One he'd made before to the cursed, but never
out loud to the Black Witch. *You'll never be able to use us for
your own purposes ever again. You want to fight your sister, do it
yourself. We are done dying for you.*

The witch scoffed at him. "Your brethren, as you call them,
don't feel the same way, I fear. You've left them with something very dangerous, dragonling. Hope. They wanted you to
free them so badly, as you promised to do. But they can all see
the evidence now that you had no intention of saving anyone
but yourself."

They wouldn't believe that.

*I have given everything to find a way to free them from your
curse.*

"Really?" Her cackle sounded like she had already won
their debate. "If that were true, you wouldn't be holding the
key to their freedom from them. You've made too many
promises you can't keep and they grow tired of waiting. Better
to stay with me and know their fates than wonder if you even
care about them."

Yvaine gasped and tried to tell him something. Even the
slightest distraction from her could give the demon dragons
the impetus needed to attack. He had to stay focused on them
if he was going to protect her. Many of them surrounding him
were restless. They looked between him and the witch. He
needed them on his side. *I keep nothing from you, brothers. I*

don't have the cure for the curse yet. I was close. I will get the unicorn's blood and save you all.

"Lies. You hold what you need in your arms now. You're just not willing to sacrifice this one insignificant creature for the legions of your brothers. They will continue to suffer and die, fighting against the dragon warriors." Ereshkigal signaled to one of the Annunaki who drew out a sword and swiped it at Jett's injured wing. He reflexively pulled it away but exposed Yvaine in the process.

The demon dragons around him snarled and hissed, jumping over themselves and each other to see her, to feel her light.

"Jett. She's right." Black swirls of Yvaine's magic drifted in and out of the tight hold he had on her. "I can help them."

No. We don't know that you can break the curse. He'd always thought he would do anything to save his brethren, it had been his only thought in everything he had done. He would sacrifice anything. Anything, except for her. He wouldn't do that. He couldn't. He would die himself first.

"But you do know it. I am evidence of that." Jett's brother walked into the cave. The demon dragons weren't surprised he was there. He must have been in communication with them when Jett threw him through the shadow into hell.

Ereshkigal took one look at the uncursed man and threw her cloak up to cover her face. She backed away and signaled to her Annunaki to use themselves as a barricade between her and his brother. In a flash, Jett realized why. His brother signaled to one group of demon dragons who turned on the Annunaki and the Black Witch. His brother was not under Ereshkigal's control and that scared her. The demon dragons didn't attack outright, instead they were coordinated, like never before, and they formed a continuous wall of fire. The two demon dragons on the outside flanks, flapped their wings at the fire and it pushed Ereshkigal and the Annunaki back.

Jett gaped at the sight of the powerful witch and her demons being repelled by an attack of such surgical precision. This was not normal behavior. Even the Black Dragon did not direct the demon dragons like this. If he had the dragon warriors might have been defeated long ago. Which made Jett wonder, did that fault lie with his father's command, or had his brethren resisted taking orders from the Black Dragon?

Ereshkigal fled the cave and Jett's mind finally felt unhindered. He could sense the thoughts of the cursed and connected with them. Most were angry with him and wanted him to give Yvaine over to them. They did believe he had tried to free them and didn't understand what was stopping him now. They couldn't understand her power over Jett.

His brother approached his hands held out like he came in peace. Jett wished that were true. "Jett, she broke the curse over me. She can save them all if you give her to us."

No. You don't know that's what changed you.

"What else could it be? Look at me. I am a man. When I shift, I am a dragon, pure in form, not some demented version tainted by the crone's demon curse." He let the dragon shimmer to the surface but did not shift.

She must have broken her spell over you too. He needed to believe that. If it had been Yvain, the implications were unbearable.

"Listen to me." Yvaine squirmed, trying to break free of his grasp. If she did and the demon dragons saw he did not have complete control over her, they would attack and he would lose her.

Shh, love.

She shook her body, fighting against him. "Don't shush me. Jett. I can help. I'm--"

He growled at them all, Yvaine, his brother, the cursed. *No.*

"We cannot wait any longer. The crone and the Black Dragon grow more desperate as the dragon warriors grow stronger these past months. We have already lost many of our brothers. The final battle is ahead and we don't need to be a part of it. Let them kill each other. Give us the girl so we can escape. Prove you are our leader and here to save us all. You will be our Wyvern and we can live out our days in peace. Because if you aren't with us, you're against us and we'll have to kill you both."

The cave around them shook and an unholy screech tore through the air. Ereshkigal dropped from the shadows on the ceiling with a dagger in each of her hands. She threw one dagger at Jett and the other at his brother. She yelled her curse at them, "*Igi hushaza hezuam! Igi hushbi ililiza hezuam!* "

Jett and his brother both fell to the ground, His body curled up into itself and his skin mottled, turning from shiny black scales to the inky oil covered skin of the demon dragon.

Yvaine dropped to her knees beside his head and touched Jett's muzzle and as if she controlled him again, he shifted into his human form. She kissed his jaw, tears streaming down her face. "Jett, what's happening?"

"Yvaine," he croaked out. It was so hard to think. "Run, hide from witch. No get you."

"She's gone. The batstriches chased her away. What did she do to you?"

His vision blurred as fire burned him from the inside out, turning his skin to blackened ash. "Curse. Demon. Me."

"Oh heck to the no. I'll break it." She grabbed the dagger

from where it had fallen to the ground beside him and held it to her wrist.

She couldn't. Jett could not let his beautiful mate sacrifice herself to try to save him. He knew what she was. He'd knows for a while, but hadn't wanted to admit it. The White Witch and the First Dragon would not give him a mate only to take her away. "No. Brothers. Kill."

But he was no child of the White Witch. It seemed she too had used him as a pawn in her war. His body shook and his muscles and bones reshaped themselves into the form of a cursed demon dragon. Soon he wouldn't care if he was a weapon or a slave. "Go. Now."

Yvaine shook her head and sliced into her arm. "I freely give to you my life's blood so that your curse may be broken forever."

The screeches and the scraping of claws of the demon dragons filled the caves, echoing off the rocks. Black shadow filled Jett's mind and the last thing he heard was the scream of a unicorn.

TEA TIME WITH THE GODDESS

*D*ragons of every color flew over head. Fire and ice blew through the air, the trees slapped batstriches, the demon dragons around, and rays of sunlight caught the beasts in mid-air turning them to puffs of smoke.

She needed to hurry and find Jett, tell him that she could break the curse. She didn't see him anywhere. "Jett. Where are you? Jett."

Yvaine? His voice was nothing more than a weak whisper in her head. *Thank the First Dragon.*

Where are you? He didn't reply. *Jett. Tell me where you are. Whatever is wrong, I can help.*

The battle raging around her faded slightly, like someone had turned down the volume on the television and put a sheer curtain in front of it. Yvaine spun in a circle trying to figure who or what had cut her off from Jett. She reached inside to see if maybe she'd done it herself by slipping into the veil, but that part of her magic wasn't there.

"Come sit by me Yvaine. Let's have a cup of tea. I find that always soothes me in times of trouble."

The innkeeper woman from the gasthaus in Germany was sitting at a little cafe table in the middle of the field where the battle was raging. She wore a flowing white dress and had little white flowers in her hair. Or maybe they were snowflakes. She poured herself a cup of tea from a fancy looking silver teapot into a very large white mug. "Sugar, dear?"

This doesn't exactly seem like the right time for a cuppa. Yvaine jerked her chin toward the sky to indicate the dragons and batstriches, the fire and ice, the full-on battle going on around their heads.

"Oh, there's always time for tea." She plopped two sugar cubes into the cup and held it out for Yvaine to take. "It's herbal. You'll like it. Nimbus clouds and mint."

Yvaine didn't know what else to do, so she tried to take the mug from the woman. Hard to do when your hands were hooves. Whoa. Again? But this didn't look like S*ìthean*, the otherworld. Cait had said that was the only time she would take her true form. The mysterious curtain must be part of the veil between the worlds. Maybe. It wasn't like the one at the abbey or when she slipped through it to transport herself out of danger.

The innkeeper blew on her cup and took a sip. She tipped her head at Yvaine, studying her. She wasn't surprised in the least by Yvaine's long white mane, pure white hide, or the frickin' horn sticking out of the middle of her forehead.

Had she also known the night Yvaine had gone to their inn? Probably. Okay, so the woman wasn't a mere innkeeper. *What do you want from me?*

The woman looked up and the sky and squinted. "You know where I think I went wrong?"

By having tea on a battlefield? Also when she magically

kidnapped people and brought them to said tea. Yvaine needed to figure out how to get away from the crazy lady and back to finding Jett. There had been something wrong with him a few minutes ago. She was sure of it, but the memory kept slipping out of place and she couldn't get a grasp on what had been happening before she found herself standing in this field.

"I've made a lot of mistakes. I'll be the first to admit it. People don't think I can do that, being a goddess and all, but I do. I screw things up all the time, you know."

I see. Why was a goddess telling her about what a screw up she was? Yvaine sniffed at her mug of tea. Probably better not to drink it.

"But somewhere along the way, I made him think that sacrifice equaled love. I don't know where I went wrong. But he's not the only one. Generations later and it's happening all over again. I didn't teach him he had inherent worth. Maybe I couldn't though. I guess that's something one has to learn for themselves." The woman stared into her teacup lost in thought. She seemed sad and Yvaine almost felt sorry for her. She must have lost someone she loved.

Someone who had sacrificed themselves for love. Who thought that's all their life was worth.

A weird pain built up in Yvaine's chest. *Who are we talking about?*

The woman sucked in a long breath and sighed, then looked over her like there hadn't even been a long lull in the conversation. "Like look at my poor little Fallyn for example."

Who is Fallyn? The one you lost? Yvaine felt like she was never getting any answers and this entire conversation was not getting her back to Jett. She needed to do that. She just couldn't remember why.

"I finally talk Kur into letting the dragons have daughters again and out she pops. She's beautiful, and sassy, and strong. A mind like a trap that one. Then I go and give her the gift of dragoness sight so she can see all the mates to come and be friends with them all and her head explodes.

What? Her head exploded? Holy crap. That was kind of a pretty bad mistake.

"For being a unicorn, you take things awfully literally, Yvaine. Fallyn's head is intact, but she's had it rough that one."

Sorry. I'm kind of new to this mythical creature thing. Fallyn is still alive then.

"Once Jett helped rescue her from hell. I have to admit, he does have the heart of a dragon. He reminds me so much of his father. All rebellious and broody. If it wasn't for his mother, I think I'd really like him. I am trying. I found you for him, didn't I?"

My Jett? All she did was ask the goddess questions. This entire conversation was so confusing. She had the feeling she was supposed to be getting something out of it. She had no idea what.

"There's only one." Duh, her tone said. "Anywhoo, now the poor thing is scared to death of the one dragon who would give anything to be with her. If she knew he was willing to die, to sacrifice his entire being to save her soul, she wouldn't want him to do that. Yet she's been doing it for him her whole life."

Sacrifice. To save a soul. A cold shiver shook her hide and her limbs went a bit numb, like they'd fallen asleep. She wasn't entirely sure they were still talking about Fallyn. *She wouldn't want that for him.*

"No." A flurry whipped through the field, sending the goddesses dress and hair into a frenzy. Her expression soured and she set down her teacup hard enough it cracked. "Let me ask you this, Yvaine. What good does it do to find your true mate and then give it all up for some noble cause?"

Gulp. *Because he'd be alive.*

"Pshhh. Not really. A piece of him would be missing. They can't live that way. They can exist, but it's a half life. It's a sad state of affairs for a dragon. Most of them don't survive." She threw her hands up in the air completely disgusted with the idea. "There's no way Fallyn would want that. I mean, would you?"

Yvaine reared up and kicked at the air. *I have to get back to him. I don't want that for Jett. I don't want that for me.*

The wind died down and the goddess poured a new cup of tea, her mug restored from the pieces she'd smashed it into. "I'm afraid you're here to stay."

No. She had to get back to Jett, back to life. Hers was just beginning. She'd gotten it all wrong. She thought if she just found out who or what she was that it would all mean something. This was all wrong. Terribly wrong. She galloped away from the goddess, through trees and over the hills. She ran and ran until she was exhausted and couldn't go anymore. She slowed to a walk. Had to keep going. The table, the tea, and the goddess reappeared in front of her and she collapsed onto the grass. Between long hard breaths she threw her questions at the woman, angry she even had to ask them. *What is this place? Why are you keeping me prisoner when I should be back there?*

The goddess took a sip of her tea. "Oh, you're dead."

Yvaine got back up and pawed at the ground. *Dead?*

She didn't feel dead. She was breathing hard, her heart beat wildly in her chest, her soul ached to be back with the one she loved. This wasn't death and she refused to be dead.

"Mostly." The goddess nodded and shrugged.

Is that even a thing?

"There's a big difference between mostly dead and all dead."

Yvaine had heard that somewhere before. *Then I can go back.*

"I can't do anything with all dead. That's not my realm. Been there, done, that. Started a war. They don't have t-shirts for that kind of thing though."

But mostly dead, Yvaine crossed her mental fingers she was right about this, *is slightly alive.*

That's how she'd been living her life. Only slightly alive. Waiting for her real life to show up. What a waste. How had she not seen that before?

The woman slow-smiled and gave Yvaine the smallest of acknowledgement nods that meant she'd given the right answer. Good. Now that they'd gotten that straight, the goddess could send her back, save her so she could start living her real life.

"I can't save you, Yvaine. Don't ask."

Oh. She totally was about to.

Save herself. If she wanted to live, she had to save herself.

Yvaine opened her eyes and closed them again. Wow. She had the worst headache. She breathed in through her nose and out through her mouth a few times trying to stave of the shooting pain in her head, her hands, her arms, her legs, her stomach. Pretty much every part of her hurt. "Ouch."

"Yvaine?"

She reopened her eyes and saw Jett, in his handsome man form, covered in silver goo. Just the man she was looking for. "You have to live."

He stopped breathing for a second and then grabbed her up in his arms. "Me? You're the one who died on me, damn it."

She breathed in his smoky scent. "Sorry about that. I know better now. Besides, I was only mostly dead." And she wasn't going to live that way anymore.

Jett held her so tight she couldn't see his face, but his body was shaking. She wanted it to be with laughter, but he was in shock. "That's not a thing."

"I think it is. I've been doing it for a while. Until I ran into you and your forced me to start living me life. Thanks for that." The goddess had said she hasn't shown that person she'd lost that he had value beyond what he could do for others. Yvaine had been on that same path. Out of anyone in the whole world, Jett should have been the one to want her to use that value to save himself and his brethren. He hadn't wanted that at all.

Jett clasped her tight in his one good arm and stood up, turning in a circle. Looking for a way out. "I'm not sure I'm the one to thank, but I'm happy to oblige you some more later. We need to get out of here now. The demon dragons are revolting. They've got Ereshkigal and the Annunaki on the run. I think her curse is breaking down. She doesn't have control over them anymore. We can escape while they're distracted."

A demon dragon whipped by them shooting fire in every direction like it was in a parade. A group of them danced in a circle around a big rock with metal handles in it. They were lashing it with their tales breaking it to bits. Oh, yeah. They were revolting all right. Like a group of teenagers whose parents were out of town for the weekend. "Jett. I want you to know that you're more than the man who has to save the demon dragons from your father. That's a great mission, but it's not going to make you whole. I know you think you're missing something inside. You're not."

The fire in his eyes flickered. "Because of you. You've shared your soul with me. I think it's what saved me from succumbing to Ereshkigal's curse again. My brother was not so lucky." He pointed to a dragon swinging from a stone stalactite in the ceiling. "Your blood alone could break the curse. But without a soulmate their demon selves took over. Your soul saved me."

"I did share my heart and soul with you, but I can't save what isn't already there. You did that. You saved yourself."

"I don't think I believe that." He stopped her from interrupting. "But I will maybe concede we saved each other together."

That would do for now. She kind of liked his theory. "What about these guys? Can we get out of here and take them with?"

"That's easier said than done. I can open the shadow, but I can't fly. My wing is still shattered. With all of them running amok, I'm afraid Cage and the dragon warriors would not take to kindly to us releasing them from hell."

Poo. "Lead them then. They've revolted against Ereshkigal, it seems like you put it in their heads that they don't have to be enslaved to the Black Dragon. All they need is someone who actually cares what happens to them to show them the way."

Jett's eyes flamed with pure blue hot flames. She watched as his mind turned the idea over in his head. He'd thought for so long that he had to free them, but they'd freed themselves. "I'm not their savior. I'm their Wyvern?"

He shook his head. Not believing his own train of thought. She kissed his jaw in her favorite spot. "Duh."

"The Wyvern." It wasn't a question this time. "Of this motley mess of half dragons. The other Wyverns will not accept them, us. We're half demon, what they've been fighting against their whole lives."

Yvaine remembered what she'd seen in the goddess's tea time. "You'll find a way to convince them. They were already prepared to fight with you. I saw them battling in the field around the abbey above ground. At least I think that's what I saw."

"We can't simply join their ranks. These guys have known nothing more than death and destruction. I can't be the Black Wyvern and think everything is going to be all hunky dory."

From out of the back of the cave and enormous dragon appeared. His scales were every color of the rainbow and he was twice as big as any other dragon Yvaine had seen. But she recognized his eyes. They were kind and had helped them before. *You're right, son. You cannot be the Black Dragon Wyvern.*

Its mental voice echoed through the cavern so loudly that every demon dragon halted in its tracks. A few hissed and screeched, flapping their wings at the big dragon. The majority of them simply stared. The dragon shook his head at them, looking slightly disgusted. *No manners, these ones. They're going to be a handful, my boy. But you'll lead them just fine.*

"You just said he wasn't the Wyvern."

The first son of the First Dragon is always the Wyvern. What I said is he isn't the Black Dragon Wyvern. Because there are no such things as black dragons.

Yvaine waved her hand around the room. "Then what are these guys?"

I believe you've been calling them batstriches. I'd like to see them be more than that. Rise up, my son.

"So you can bring the Black Dragon down to kill me and

take over his Wyr? He is your son, isn't he?" Jett snarled and his dragon shimmered to the surface. He clasped Yvaine's hand in his, grounding himself to her.

He is. He is the first-born dragon of mine and Inanna's. But he isn't the first son of the First Dragon. He has no claim to the Demon Dragon Wyr. Before I met Inanna, or rather, before she fought her sister and saved me from the depths of this hell, I had another son. The product of my union with a Galla Demon. Your mother.

The big dragon, who Yvaine now understood must be the First Dragon blew a swirl of rainbow-colored fire into the cavern, lighting each of the demon dragons on fire. But they didn't erupt into flames, they grew and stretched their wings and transformed into big black dragons with fiery eyes, almost identical to Jett's.

You aren't the Black Wyvern, my son. You're the Demon Dragon Wyvern.

*Y*ou are the Demon Dragon Wyvern.

The words played over and over in Jett's head.

The Demon Dragon Wyvern.

Demon Dragon.

Wyvern.

The first son of the First Dragon.

The first son.

"Jett?"

He should probably be doing something, saying something. He couldn't seem to get his arms or legs or anything else to work. Yeah, some great Wyvern he was going to be, frozen in place by fear in hell. The brothers he'd known in their withered forms no longer squawked and hissed. A thousand mental voices filled his head until he couldn't hear his own thoughts.

...you're more than the man who has to save the demon dragons...

"I think they're all waiting for you to say something since you dad just up left in a poof of rainbow sparkles."

Yeah. They probably were waiting for him to say or do something. Hell if he knew what. He didn't know anything about being a leader. Where would they live. Who was going to teach them all about how to control the shadow? How many dragon warriors would they have to fight before--

Yvaine grabbed his cheeks in her hands and yanked his head down to hers. She planted her lips on his and snuck her tongue inside his mouth before he even finished his dark thoughts. He resisted her for a split second before closing his eyes, threading his good arm into her hair and kissing her like his life depended on it.

It did.

The good part of his life anyway. The part he wanted to live with her. "Yvaine."

"There you are. I like it when you growl my name. It's very sexy."

"What would I do without you?" She could maintain that she hadn't saved him, but he would always believe that without her he'd still be slumming it in some bar waiting for the cure for all his ails to simply appear. She changed everything and made him want to be a better man. A better dragon. A better demon dragon.

She smiled up at him and patted his cheek. "Apparently stand around with your thumb up your butt. Hey, if you're like the king now, does that mean I get a crown?"

He scanned the room and saw his Wyr, each and every one of them also trying to figure out what had just happened. All but one. The brother who'd first broken Ereshkigal's curse. Maybe with Yvaine's blood, maybe not. "You can have whatever you want, love."

Yvaine traced the path he was staring and pulled away. Too bad. "Maybe after we get out of hello kitty."

"Really? Hell is one of the words you can't say. It's just a place." Granted one laced with evil, tortured souls, and destruction.

She shrugged.

Two demon dragons scuffled in one corner of the cave drawing Jett's attention away from his lovely soul mate's lips. He supposed if he left the demon dragons to their own devices much longer they would all start getting ideas about fighting for dominance. He needed to establish the hierarchy and a chain of command now so they knew where they stood and what they could and could not do in this new world they were all living in.

He cleared his throat and opened his mind to all of them. When he spoke there was a new tone to his voice. One of the alpha. "Brothers. The tide of our fortunes has changed, thanks in part to your determination to throw off the yoke of Ereshkigal's spell. The First Dragon has granted us a new lease on life. I cannot promise it will be easy. We will have to find a different way of living than any of us have ever known before. I swear to you that I will do everything in my power to make sure you each get a fair shake, but there will be no hand-outs from me or the dragon warriors. Each of you will have to work for everything you need."

Several demon dragons stepped forward and shifted into human forms. They looked surprised at first that they had the power to assume these new forms, then the first one spoke. "What about mates. How did you steal the soul to get yours? Will you teach us?"

"No." There were so many growls from the demon dragons the room vibrated with the noise. "Because I won't need to. We were taught by Ereshkigal and the Black Dragon that we were soulless. They were wrong."

More demon dragons shifted. "But we do not have shards like the dragon warriors. How do we know we have souls?"

Good questions. Jett took Yvaine's hand and thought carefully about how she'd helped him understand that his own life had that inherent value. It wasn't her words, although they'd helped drive it home. It was the way she'd simply believed in him all along. "Look inside yourselves, that glimmer of magic, the part that you can feel the shadow moving within, the piece of you that says live, damn it, live. That is how you know you have a soul."

Some of the demon dragons nodded, understanding. Many more scowled at him. It would take time for them to believe their lives were worth living, that the worthlessness that had been beaten into them for so long was wrong.

"And mates?" His brother stepped to the front of the pack. The fire in his eyes burned with a covetous light at Yvaine. She didn't flinch. Jett wanted to. He didn't want anyone thinking about her in any way other than as mate to their Wyvern. Except he'd probably looked at Azy and Ciara the same way. Without having seen how a mate had changed Cage and Jakob, Jett might not have wanted one of his own. His Yvaine was the shining light of promise to each of the demon dragons that there could be someone who loved them out there in the world too. He could not deny them that.

"How will we get shards of our souls to give to them. We've all seen the dragon warrior's shards glow when they are with their mate. They give that piece of their souls over to their mate for safe keeping. We don't have that. How will we know?"

"You'll know. Trust me. You'll know. We are not the same as the dragon warriors. We will have to figure out what is right for our Wyr, together." That seemed to appease the majority for now. He answered a few more questions, one about names that he couldn't answer for them. He didn't know where he'd gotten his own name, only that he had one.

Yvaine supplied the answer. "It will be a rite of passage for you all to choose a name for yourself."

His brother, still at the front of the group turned and addressed the Wyr. "I have been in the world in this form and I choose for myself the name Neo."

A fine choice. "Neo, stand before me in fealty. I name you the second to the Wyvern. Should I ever fall in battle, you will lead our brethren."

Neo stood tall and took Jett's arm and hand, clasping them. "Thank you, brother. I accept."

"Excellent. Your first duty as my second is to find us a place to live. I am tired of the depths of hell. Let the shadow guide you." Neo raised his eyebrow, jerked back and touched his forehead, clearly surprised his face had moved in that way. Jett clapped him on the back. "Choose some lieutenants too. We need to organize this exodus out of hell."

Neo pointed to a few of the demon dragon men in the front row to come forward. "What of the dragon warriors. Won't they attack when they see so many of us rising from here?"

Jett nodded. He'd been thinking the same thing. He would seek out Cage first as the AllWyvern of the dragon warriors. "I've got some favors owed from them. I'll be using those to call an AllWyr. Soon enough the other Wyverns will have to learn of and accept our new status."

"Good luck with that."

He was going to need it.

They spent the next several hours organizing the demon dragons into groups with varying tasks. Jett spent most of his time teaching individuals how to harness the shadow to they could pass through it. Yvaine tended to the wounds of many of them. She discovered after she sneezed on one of them that it wasn't only her blood that had magical powers, but her saliva too. Old wounds were healed and those who'd had trouble shifting between dragon and human form could move between the two easily after she licked her hand and touched them. She was with one small group of them who were making her laugh so hard she was crying and when she wiped a tear from her face Jett excused himself to join them.

He hadn't expected any of them to have a sense of humor. He'd been in a dark place for a long time after his own spell had been broken that he thought they would all be broody and cranky too. But each of his demon dragons were reacting to the transition in their own ways. It would take him some time to start thinking of them all as individuals and not the one big hive mind he was used to.

"Let me see your finger, love." There was something about her slivery tears he didn't want to share with anyone else. She could sneeze or spit on whoever she wanted to, but her tears of joy were his and his alone.

He brought her hand to his mouth and sucked the little tear drop from the end. A burst of tingling excitement shot from his tongue, through his core and straight to his cock. Yep. He'd thought as much. Those tears were his.

"I think we've done enough for today. You've healed many demon dragons and it's time I took you someplace to get some rest." Or to get busy.

Yvaine's eyes sparkled but she didn't take his bait. "I've healed pretty much everyone except for you. Come here. Let me see your arm. You should have let me look at it sooner."

"There were others for you to help first. I don't want the others to think I garner special treatment."

"I know one kind of special treatment you get from me that they don't." She pulled him in for a good long kiss and funny how his arm suddenly felt better.

Jett glanced at his arm and saw a smear of silver that streaked from his shoulder to his wrist. If he never saw Yvaine's blood again, it would be too soon. "You tricked me."

"I did." She grinned up at him and stuck the end of her finger in her mouth soothing the tiny hole he couldn't figure out how she'd made in her skin. "But it was worth it. A tiny prick to my finger didn't do me any harm and it did you a lot of good. I want every single bit of you in working order, mister."

Jett hugged Yvaine to him, holding her tight and whispered in her here. "You've healed me for your own selfish reasons, have you?"

She ran her hands into his hair and guided his mouth down to the shimmering black and red dragon mark on her neck. He obliged with a scrape of his teeth across her skin. "If wanting your hands down my pants is selfish, then yes."

Okay, foreplay was over. He wanted to get her to a bed ASAP. But he didn't have a home for her yet. Hmm. "Neo. We're going to the Green Wyvern's villa to work out details of a treaty with them. You're in charge while we're gone."

"Yes, sir." Neo gave him a little salute and went back to conferring with the group around him.

Jett opened his senses and called up a bit of shadow just large enough for the two of them to pass through. He opened his wings and let a warm current guide them through the darkness. It was lazy and perfect because it gave him time to kiss Yvaine senseless while putting his hands all over her body, getting her all hot and bothered.

"Oh my goodness. Do that thing with your tongue again." She groaned against him and wrapped her legs around his waist.

"As you wish, love."

The sound of a throat being cleared tried it's best to break into Jett's living fantasy. "Ahem."

He had the strangest sense of deja vu and very gently broke the kiss, but moved his lips only far enough away from hers to speak. "Go away. We're busy."

"Ah, Ah, Ahem."

This person did not understand they were endangering their own life. "What part of go away don't you understand?"

"You're the one standing in my living room on the verge of sexing up Yvaine. I'm not going anywhere. I'll stay and watch the show." The pure enjoyment of irritating Jett was rife in Ciara's voice.

"I personally would prefer if you took your mate to the bedroom we provided you and returned when you were suitably satisfied and clothed." Jakob always was a spoilsport.

Yvaine peeked over Jett's shoulder. "Give us a few hours and then we can do the whole mimosa gossip thing again. Have I got a lot to dish about."

Jett set Yvaine gently on the plush carpet of the Green Wyvern's living room and turned to address Jakob. "Give us until the morning, and then I declare an AllWyvern to discuss the matter of the Demon Dragon Wyr."

Jakob held up his hand, but Ciara grabbed it and held it to her chest before her mate could flip his shit. That's what the look on his face said he was ready to do. Thank goodness for Ciara and her powers. "Yep. We'll see you in the morning.

Night, night. Sleep tight. Don't let the dragons bite. Unless that turns you on and in that case, have at it."

"Miláček." Jakob grumbled, but Jett did not stick around long enough to see if this lovers quarrel ended up in the bedroom or not. He had his own mate to attend to.

Jett pulled her toward the stairs. His cock was already pushing against the seam of his jeans and they'd be lucky to make it to the hallway before he threw her up against the wall and fucked her. Light flashed around them and all of a sudden they were standing in the bedroom.

"Sorry, I couldn't wait and dragged us through the veil to get us here faster. I didn't think you'd mind," Yvaine said. She grabbed his t-shirt and pulled it over his head and then went straight for his jeans. "I need you naked right now."

He wasn't as patient as she was and he shredded her clothes so that she was bare for him in an instant. Later he would take his time kissing and sucking and licking every one of her lush curves. He was going to spend a very long time worshipping her ass. First, he was going to sate both of them with a hard, fast fuck. "On the bed, Yvaine on your hands and knees."

"A. Quit tearing my clothes. Do you know how hard it is to find t-shirts with unicorns on them in my size? Not to mention XXL panties that aren't plain white or tan."

"I will buy you a whole unicorn clothing factory if you like, mate. Because there will never be a time where I don't want to rip your clothes off and have you naked."

The sparkle in her eyes told him she liked that answer. Good. Because if he could he would have her naked and all to himself all the time."

"Fine, and B. Are you going to spank me? That sounds like a lot of fun."

It did in fact sound like fun. How she knew about kinky fuckery though, he didn't know. Oh. Right. She'd mentioned something before. "Remind me to also buy stock in those romance novels of yours."

Lots and lots of stock.

LOVE AND OTHER BUTT STUFF

*O*h em gee oh dee. Yvaine's insides turned all mushy when Jett got bossy. Watching him assume the role of Wyvern and stepping into that role he was so obviously born for had her heart going pitter patter all day long. Now that she had him alone and mostly naked she was going to have her way with him. Just as soon as he had his way with her.

She hopped up on the bed, exactly like he asked and wiggled her butt at him. She'd been a little busy in the past couple of days and had not gotten a chance to check out any naughty romance novels. He was just going to have to teach her about the butt stuff.

Thwack. His hand landed on the back of her right thigh and she nearly came off the bed. Not because it hurt, but because it warmed her up from the inside out. "Do it again."

She heard his jeans drop to the floor and felt the bed dip behind her as he crawled on behind her. Thwack. He smacked the other one and then rubbed his hand over the sting. That was even more incredible.

"Why didn't you do this to me last time we had sex?"

Jett didn't reply with words, nope. He shoved her shoulders down so her face was buried in the pillows and her ass was still stuck straight up in air waiting for more of his attention. Thwack, thwack, thwack.

Her rear was on fire and it was melting her between her legs. "More Jett. It's getting me so hot for you."

She waited for another spanking but instead he got his hot breath over her already heated skin. "I like to see how your skin glows for me. Let's see how it tastes." He kissed the small of her back and worked his way down her right butt cheek. She hissed when he pressed his mouth against her tight hole. He only teased her with that kiss and continued down to where his spanking stung the most. He soothed the stings with his tongue and worked his way between her thighs.

"Spread your legs wider for me so I can lick and suck your pretty pink pussy. I want to hear you come hard with my tongue inside of your." He didn't wait for her to follow his direction and pushed her legs apart for her. He teased her clit with his tongue and then delved inside of her mimicking the in and out thrusts of sex.

Yvaine gripped the pillows and groaned out his name. "Jett. Ah, yes. Oh. Oh that feels so good."

He slid his hand between her legs and fingered her clit fast and hard while not letting up with his thrusts and sucks and licks. That plus the heat of his spankings and the second he growled against her, she exploded into what she hoped was the first of a whole lot of climaxes. She barely caught her breath before Jett was up and behind her pushing his hips against her ass.

"Don't move, Yvaine. I need to take you fast and hard again. You drive me crazy. I want to take it slow with you, make it the beautiful thing you deserve, but I can't." He growled again as he pushed into her, taking her all the way in one long hard stroke. He filled her so completely and she never felt better than when he was inside of her.

"Do it. Don't make me say it, just. Do. It." Yvaine tilted her pelvis back, sliding him in even deeper and they both lost their minds from the rush of pleasure.

Jett pulled back and slammed back into her. "This cunt is mine. All mine. I'm going to claim it and you over and over. No dragon or demon will ever wonder whose scent is on you. I'm going to fuck you so much that no one will know the difference between where I end and you begin."

He grabbed her hips and set up a pace that had her crying out his name in long low guttural groans. This was exactly what she wanted from him. The two of them together, fulfilling each other's needs not only in the bedroom but in each other's hearts.

Jett reached around and stroked her clit again without stopping the in and out pistoning of his hips. She was already climbing toward her next orgasm and it didn't take but a few of his touches to send her careening over the edge. Her entire body shook with the power of this one and her muscles clenched around Jett's body inside of hers.

"Fuck, yes, Yvaine, milk my cock. God, I love coming inside of you." His hips jerked and she felt him spill his seed deep into her.

They collapsed together on the bed, his body still inside of hers, his massive shoulders and arms covering hers. Jett groaned and rolled off of her too soon for her liking but pulled her to him and wrapped them up in his wings. She loved this dark cocoon he created for them. It made her feel like they were the only two people in the world.

They slept, made love again, this time on the fuzzy carpet in front of the fireplace. And then over the back of the couch. And then up against the door. And one more time back in the bed.

Yvaine almost drifted off to sleep in his arms again but pulled herself awake to ask him something very important. "Will you marry me?"

He stroked her back for a moment before answering. "I will do the human custom if it makes you happy. But Yvaine, you're not actually human. We don't need their papers and customs."

It wasn't the piece of paper she wanted. "I know, but all my memories are of growing up human. I want to do some of those things. With you."

A knock sounded at their door. "Did somebody mention a wedding?"

Jett's eyes popped open and he glared at the door. "Ciara, go away. Have you been listening this whole time?"

"No," she squeaked.

Totally.

"Liar." He shouted back at her. "Jakob needs to find something productive for his mate to do."

Yvaine could practically hear Ciara huff. She shouted through the door again and wiggled the door handle. They'd remembered to lock it sometime in the past twenty-seven orgasms. "Planning a wedding is productive."

Another voice came through the door. "So is planning an AllWyr, Ciara. Leave the rogue and his mate alone, or you'll be getting spankings of your own."

Their voices faded off but Yvaine still caught Ciara's purr. "Yeah, because that's going to be a real punishment, Jakob.

"Are they always like that?" Yvaine didn't remember having

friends before. She understood there were other dragons' mates and couldn't wait to meet them. Well, she could wait until morning because she had more plans for the evening activities of her mate.

"Yes." He sighed but then rolled over and pulled her on top of him.

"I like them."

"I like you better."

He showed her just how much he liked her then. For the twenty-eighth time. And the twenty-ninth, and the thirtieth.

Morning came all too early but Yvaine was starving and dragged Jett down to the kitchen. Ciara was there with two other women and two toddlers.

"Oh here they are. Jada, Azy, meet Yvaine."

They exchanged pleasantries and she got to coo at how adorable Azy's children were before the men joined them. Man alive, there had to be a thing that all dragon dudes were hawt. She already knew how good-looking Cage and Jakob were, but Jett had to lift her chin shut when she got a look at Jada's mate, Ky.

Yvaine pulled on Jett's ear. "We are definitely going to visit them in New Zealand. It sounds like a great place for the Demon Dragon's home to be."

"No." That's all he said but gave Ky a little glare.

Cage announced that the AllWyr was set for that evening. "We're just waiting on Match."

Jett looked uncomfortable at the mention of that other dragon. She took his hand and rubbed her thumb over the back of it to soothe him. "Okay, good then we can plan the wedding in the meantime. I'd like it to be totally normal, white dress, flowers, cake, and lots of guests."

"But, being normal is so boring, sweet child." Tea time

goddess/innkeeper/lady in white strolled into the kitchen. She wore those same flowing white robes, had flowers in her hair that still reminded Yvaine of what Mother Nature would look like if she was also Aphrodite.

Ciara got out some tea cups even though they were about to have her famous mimosas. "Oh, hello Mrs. Bohacek. I wondered when you might show up."

"Hello, Ciara. How is you magic coming along? I'm only here for a second. The love of my life asked me to stop by and give Yvaine this." The woman slid a thick padded envelope onto the counter and then was gone.

"What do you suppose is in this?" Yvaine picked up the envelope and slit the seal to open it. There was a small black velvet box inside. She tipped the envelope up and the box dropped into her hand.

Azy looked at her strangely. "What's that. Where did that envelope come from?"

Weird. "The lady Ciara called Mrs. Bohacek was just here and gave it to me."

"She was. Funny. I haven't seen her in forever." Jada opened up a box of homemade donuts and picked one out for each of them.

Yvaine gave each of the ladies a touch on the head to see if they were feeling alright. "By forever do you mean one minute ago?"

"Mrph, nope." Jada said with her mouth full. Girl after Yvaine's own heart, that one.

She looked over at each of the dragon warriors. "You saw her, didn't you?"

They each shook their heads.

"Jett? Please tell me I'm not crazy."

He grinned at her and fed her a bit of one of Jada's

donuts. "You're not. They don't see her or remember her if she doesn't want them to. I think it has something to do with her being a great, great something or other ancestor of theirs."

"Do you mean the White Witch?" Ciara asked.

"I have no idea. But she just gave me this. Does that answer the question?" Yvaine popped the box open and found a ring inside. But this was no ordinary ring. It looked like it was made of smoke or rather, shadow. The darkness undulated and moved in swirling circles. But every so often a red spark would go off inside making the whole ring shine like it was filled with a million embers.

Ciara gawked at the ring inside the box. "Oh my gods and goddesses. Do you know what that is?"

"A ring?" Seemed pretty obvious.

Azy glanced over at Cage. "It's a Wyvern's mates ring."

Cool. She was a Wyvern's mate after all. But the way they were all looking shell shocked it must have more significance than that. "What does that mean?"

Ciara stared at the ring, then at Jett, then at Yvaine. "Mates of Wyverns have to prove to the Wyr and to the other Wyvern's that she is worthy of being mated to a leader of the dragon warriors. The biggest part of that is a trial where the White Witch hides a ring that she has to find. Only when she does can they be officially mated and recognized as his true mate."

Cage shook his head. "I like you and all Jett and you're a great warrior, but there are only four Wyrs."

A super handsome guy walked into the kitchen. He smelled of smoke and Jett squeezed her hand. "Not anymore. We must recognize the Demon Dragons as our brothers. Jett has proven himself to be a leader."

Cage met this new guy with a handshake. "Match, you're here earlier than expected. Did you find Fallyn?"

Ooh. Yvaine new that name, but she didn't know who it was. She leaned over to Jett and quietly asked him. "Who is Fallyn?"

He hadn't yet taken his eyes off the new guy. The red fire in his eyes was getting stoked up and not in the good way. "The Black Dragon's daughter."

"So, your sister?" He should have mentioned if he had some other siblings.

He shook his head "No. I'll explain it later."

They'd missed part of the conversation between Cage and new guy, but they didn't look like there had been good news.

Cage spoke to new guy, but it was clear he was addressing the room. "This war has gone on long enough. I'm going to end it one way or another. Now that you've broken the curse, Jett. We welcome you into the AllWyr. The Black Dragon and Ereshkigal are weakened. Now is the time to strike."

Jett stood and pulled Yvaine up with him. "I appreciate your welcome brothers. But the Demon Dragon Wyr has a long road ahead and much to learn. Now is not the time to force them into battle."

Cage did not like that. Yvaine saw him stiffen and something change in his stance. She recognized the move from when Jett had taken on the mantle of Wyvern. She held up her hand and let a little of the magic between her and Jett flow into the room. That got everyone's attention. She nodded to Jett and he squeezed her hand.

"I will not force my Wyr into battle, but we can still help. The demon dragons can pass through the shadow. We will be your eyes and ears and get you intel on the Ereshkigal, the Black Dragon and his troops that are not a part of my Wyr.

Bring me to the Annunaki and I will also tell you where Gesh-tianna is hiding."

The air in the room stilled and all eyes flicked between Cage and Jett. Match put a hand on Cage's shoulder. "Can your demon dragons also help me find Fallyn."

Jett nodded. "They can try. But she is as smart or smarter than anyone I know. It won't be easy."

"I understand." An anger and then sadness flickered across Match's face.

Cage outstretched his hand to Jett and everyone around them breathed a sigh of relief. Jett took it and the two shook. A burst of gold light shimmered in the air over their hands and was joined with swirls of black. The deal was done.

Yvaine clapped because it seemed appropriate and it broke the tension in the room. "Now that that's all settled can we get down to the mimosas? I have some girl talk questions I'd like to ask the other mates."

Cage and Match slowly backed away and Jakob led Ky out the opposite door. Jett didn't get to escape because Yvaine snagged the back of his t-shirt.

"Ciara. Tell him that girls like butt stuff."

Ciara spit her mimosa out and had to wipe the counter up with a paper towel. "Umm. I am not getting involved in this one."

She pointed at Jett. "You are sticking it in my butt."

Jett raised one eyebrow and that blue flame lit in his eyes. The really hot one. Either he was turned on or mad or both.

He took one long strides across the room and picked her up, throwing her over his shoulder. "Ciara, please excuse my mate's crudeness. I apologize if she has shocked or offended any of you."

The girls all laughed conspiratorially and Yvaine liked

them even more. Especially Azy because she said, "No, it's okay. Also, FYI, she's right. Women do like it."

Jett dragged her back upstairs and away from the girl talk. Where they did indeed try butt stuff.

Laying again in his arms, wrapped in his wings, Yvaine had never been happier. "Jett?"

"Yes, love."

"Wanna make babies?"

Jett rolled her over and buried his face against the dragon mark on her neck. It wasn't an answer, but it made her happy anyway.

IF YOU HAVEN'T READ the book that started it all, check out Chase Me where you'll get to read about Jakob Zeleny, the Green Dragon Wyvern, and his mate Ciara's love adventure. You can binge read dragon shifters and their curvy mates for days!

If you're all caught up with the dragons, you might like my other shifter series – Fated For Curves. Book one, *A Touch of Fate* stars a curvy geek girl and a bear-shifter space ranger who are out to save the world from the scourge of soul stealing spectrals.

Grab A Touch of Fate today.

Keep reading for a letter from me, the author, for you, the reader, about what's coming next in the Dragons Love Curves series.

A LETTER FROM THE AUTHOR

Who loves Dragons?

Dear reader,

I hope you loved reading this adventure in the Dragons Love Curves series with Jett and Yvaine!

Sometimes the dragons and their mates surprise even me.

I've got some fun surprises coming in the next books in the Dragons Love Curves series, so be sure to follow me on Amazon, Bookbub, Facebook, or my Curvy Connection to find out what happens next (hint: Jett, who doesn't have a soul shard and has decided he doesn't need one anyway is in for one wild ride.)

Stay tuned to get your fix of sexy dragon shifters giving their mates happy ever afters (and happy endings! Lol)

I'd love if you left a review for this story. I really appreciate you telling other readers what you thought and how the book made you FEEL!

Even if you're not sure what to say – it can be as simple as

– "Read this in one sitting." or "Hooray for curvy girls and dragons." Just one sentence will do a lot.

Do you need more curvy girls getting their happy ever afters?

Want to be the first to know when the next book comes out (plus get cool exclusive content from me!)? Sign up for my Curvy Connection mailing list. Go here http://geni.us/CurvyConnection to sign up and I'll send you another curvy girl romance right away to say thanks for joining me!

Find me at www.AidyAward.com or on Facebook, Twitter, Instagram, or follow me on BookBub.

Kisses,

~Aidy

ALSO BY AIDY AWARD

The Curvy Love Series

Curvy Diversion

Curvy Temptation

Curvy Persuasion

Curvy Domination (coming soon)

The Curvy Seduction Saga

Rebound

Rebellion

Reignite

Dragons Love Curves

Chase Me

Tease Me

Bite Me

Cage Me

Baby Me

Defy Me

More dragons coming soon!

Fated for Curves

A Curvy Girl Sci-fi Romance Series

A Touch of Fate

A Tangled Fate

A Twist of Fate

More Space Rangers coming soon!

ABOUT THE AUTHOR

Aidy Award is a curvy girl who kind of has a thing for stormtroopers. She's also the author of the popular Curvy Love series and the hot new Dragons Love Curves series. She writes curvy girl erotic romance, about real love, and dirty fun, with happy ever afters because every woman deserves great sex and even better romance, no matter her size, shape, or what the scale says.

Read the delicious tales of hot heroes and curvy heroines come to life under the covers and between the pages of Aidy's books. Then let her know because she really does want to hear from her readers.

Connect with Aidy on her website. www.AidyAward.com get her Curvy Connection, and join her Facebook Group - Aidy's Amazeballs.

Printed in Great Britain
by Amazon